AT HIS COUNTESS' PLEASURE

OLIVIA WAITE

CONTENT NOTE

Part of this story's plot centers around infertility and childlessness. I can think of a hundred reasons why someone might choose to avoid these topics: if you need to, you have my full support to set this book aside unread.

CHAPTER 1

*M*iss Anne Pym kept her eyes fixed on Rushmore House as she stepped out of the carriage. The building in front of her was white marble, gleaming in the pale winter sunlight like an ancient matriarch. Amazing how time could be so kind to a building, yet so unkind to a gown—Anne's pale pink muslin had seen only three years to compare to the great house's three decades, but where Rushmore House had silvered over with dignity, the gown had only faded and aged. Nevertheless, Anne strode bravely up the walkway while her maid Dorothy fluttered behind her like an errant handkerchief. The butler who answered Anne's knock raised an eyebrow at her appearance, but admitted her and offered to show her to the parlor to wait.

"No, thank you," said the lady, "I shall see the earl at once, please."

Gently but firmly, the butler denied her.

Anne swept by him and ascended the stairs. The butler abandoned the maid in the foyer and followed Anne, pleading in increasingly strident tones.

Her feet never faltered.

Though she had only been here twice before, Anne knew the

way to the study. The door was open, so she sailed over the threshold without a pause and curtsied with all propriety to the man seated there.

Simon Rushmore, Earl of Underwood, rose from his desk and waved his butler into silence. "Thank you, Phillips," he said, not without sympathy. "Would you have Cook send up some tea for our guest?"

"No tea, thank you," said Anne.

The earl nodded acquiescence. Phillips bowed, spots of red staining his decorous cheeks, and the door closed whisper-soft behind him.

The earl tilted his head at Anne, clearly bemused. "To what do I owe the honor, Miss Pym?"

Anne had prepared herself for precisely this moment. She folded her hands in front of her and said, "I have come, my lord, for restitution."

The earl's eyebrows lifted.

Anne didn't wait for him to ask her to explain further. "Your brother did a great injury to my family when he seduced my cousin Hecuba and painted her...*en deshabille*," she said.

The earl sighed, not as though he'd forgotten the incident, but as though it weighed heavily on him. "He did indeed, Miss Pym, but they are married now. Surely honor has been satisfied?"

Anne had anticipated this denial and was determined to challenge it. "Your honor may be, but ours is still tarnished. John and Hecuba only married after the scandal had run its course. There was a full month of the Season when we were all quite thoroughly shunned—left isolated, disgraced and avoided by anyone of name." And now that Hecuba had opened her shop and was selling paints to artists all over Britain, last year's scandal had new life on the lips of society's gossips this spring. *A cousin in trade! Can you credit it? Who would invite her anywhere, if not to gawk?* Anne realized her hands were twisting nervously together and set them into fists instead. "My cousin's marriage to your brother may have made them both deliriously happy, but it has done nothing to restore my family's social standing."

The earl grimaced, but he nodded. Quite as though she'd said something ordinary and reasonable. Anne allowed a small seed of hope to begin sprouting. "What do you suggest I do about it?" he asked. One corner of his mouth quirked up. "I assume you came here with a practical scheme in mind."

She had, and she was frank enough to admit it. "It's nothing so terrible. All I ask is that you host a few dinners, maybe a party or two, and invite us as well as your usual circle. My younger sister is pretty and charming and perfectly capable of attaching some eligible gentleman. She had a few excellent prospects last Season —I'm sure it would not take long for one of those attachments to rekindle. If she were given the opportunity."

His eyes were cool and considering. "And what of yourself, Miss Pym?"

The question hit a sore spot, pressing her lips into a thin line. Anne was realistic about her own capacity to allure. She had excellent posture and straight teeth and no noticeable blemishes on her skin, but no artist would ever beg to paint her portrait. She had eyes that could see well enough and a mouth that could form words and a nose that perched on her face as it was supposed to. As much as she had once wished otherwise, Anne Pym was as plain and serviceable as the brown woolen gowns she'd left behind her in the countryside.

She knew what she was. But more importantly, she knew what she wanted.

"I want a family," Anne said. "I want a husband who is kindhearted and who gives me at least three children. I want to have money enough to keep fed and warm in the winter, and not to have to worry about how to pay the cook's wages or buy new clothes for the children when they outgrow the old. I know something about money worries, my lord. My father has just enough funds left to give us one more Season in town, and I mean to make the most of it. It's possible there are men I knew in the country with whom I could be happy, but I would prefer to spread as wide a net as possible, the better to increase the odds." She caught her breath, having admitted more than she'd intended. It was hard not to when he was looking at her with such thoughtfulness. As if he were really listening. As if what she was saying were important. She was unused to the weight of true attention, and for the first time in her quest she hesitated. "This may strike you as being tawdry or mercenary, my lord, but I am an essentially practical person, and I suspect you value frankness highly enough to excuse any indelicacy of expression." *That's enough, Anne,* she told herself, and clamped her mouth shut.

He watched her for a while longer, then drew himself up, hands behind his back. The pose broadened his shoulders in a way that sent a quiet pulse through Anne's veins. The earl blushed only slightly and said: "Miss Pym, would you consider marrying me?"

Anne blinked. This she had not anticipated.

To give herself time to think about how to respond, she turned a critical eye upon the earl's person. Lord Underwood was only a few inches taller than she was. He was neither fat nor thin—he was simply solid, his body a set of straight up-and-down lines like a tree trunk that had access to an excellent tailor. He had a square face, held in place by a lumpy nose and weighed down by a stern chin. His eyes were dark and his hair plain brown, with a moustache that could just be termed elegant. He stood patiently beneath her examination and waited for her conclusions.

Physical charms aside, from his behavior after her cousin's seduction and marriage Anne knew that he had a steely sense of right and wrong and preferred to deal with problems in a head-on, forthright manner. This was someone she could lean on, yes—but he was also someone she could quarrel with if there came a need.

She came to a quick decision. "I would indeed consider marrying you, my lord," Anne said. "But I would also like to know why you should consider marrying me."

"Ah." Lord Underwood smiled and his shoulders relaxed. "Since my brother wed, I have been thinking it is time I started a family of my own. An earl needs an heir, and since John and Hecuba moved out, the house has had an empty rattle to it. I admire your character and the fact that you are moved to pursue what you want. It strikes me that this would be a fine quality in a wife—in a countess, especially—and in the mother of my children. More personally, I think we would suit well enough—and I don't feel particularly inclined to throw my heart upon the tender bosom of society. To parade myself before a host of strange and pale young misses, gouty fathers, and overeager mothers." Anne, whose mother could well be encompassed by the term *overeager*, grimaced in sympathy. The earl leaned forward, resting one hand on the desk. "Allow me to make my case to you. My fortune more than meets the requirements you listed, and three children strikes me as an excellent number to have. Your gaining the title of countess would redeem your family's reputation at once, particularly since you and I would not have an initial scandal to overcome. In short," the earl concluded, "your problem and mine could be most speedily solved if we marry." He nodded, as though the gesture might convince her if his arguments had not.

His logic appeared sound, but... "Are you always this...efficient?" Anne asked.

"No," the earl admitted, mouth quirking. "Nor always so nonchalant. I can be a little irritable at times. I have my whimsical moods, the same as any man." He glanced away briefly, then brought those gray eyes back to meet hers. "But I feel very strongly that opportunities should be seized when they present themselves."

Anne nodded in approval. This was entirely in line with her own philosophy. She had always listened to her instincts, and they were speaking quite loudly at the moment. "I think we may do very well together, my lord," she said. "Would you care to call tomorrow at tea to propose formally? I can guarantee my father will be at home."

"It will be a pleasure, Miss Pym," said the earl, and held out a hand.

They shook, and the bargain was sealed.

Simon walked Miss Pym to the door, admiring the way she held her head high and her shoulders straight beneath the faded cloth of her dress. The immoveable Phillips reddened at once when he saw her—a minor miracle, which boded well for her future as mistress of the house—and both Miss Pym and her anxious maid were quickly shown into their carriage. Simon then ordered his own equipage readied, as he had a rather delicate errand to run.

If he was to be married, he would need to break with his mistress.

Perhaps it wasn't something every gentleman would do, but it felt...well, *impolite* to divide his energies between the beds of two separate women. Especially since only one of them would be fully aware of the arrangement. Once he and Anne had produced a few children, he might begin another discreet liaison, but for at least his first two years as a husband, it seemed only correct to devote every iota of his marital attentions to his wife.

He would miss Fiona, though: her gold-blonde hair, her easy comfort, the warm lush weight of her in bed. She'd indulged both his physical desires and his intellectual ones: they'd had tea and conversation at least as often as they'd fucked. He decided to settle an annuity on her, to ensure she would have a source of income throughout her life even after her looks had left her. He'd heard of other men doing similar things, and it had always struck him as a particularly civilized gesture. He might stop by the jeweler's on the way, too, and pick up something pretty as a parting gift. She would like that. Diamonds were too pale to suit her—perhaps something in sapphires?

~

The ceremony had been performed and the register signed. Thanks to the warm gold band on her finger, plain Anne Pym was now the Right Honorable Anne Rushmore, Countess of Underwood.

It had not been a lengthy engagement. Banns had been read and relatives informed. Anne was dressed in pale yellow, a color she loathed. But it had been the only dress in her wardrobe she hadn't worn yet, and she hadn't wanted to waste the money on a new one, not when her family still had one younger daughter to clothe. Anne would buy new gowns when she was a countess and could afford them.

The wedding breakfast was small but splendid. White soup and eggs and bread and bacon, lobster and potatoes and kippers and ham. Coffee, tea, and chocolate warmed in gleaming silver vessels. The guests crowded into the Pym parlor were limited to family—though Anne did wish Hecuba could have been there. Anne's mother had nearly had an apoplexy at the mere suggestion, however, and the bride had reluctantly yielded to propriety. Besides, if her mother found it shocking, others would too, and the purpose of this wedding was to dampen shock, not to excite it.

At least she was free to be intrigued by Simon's aunt and cousin, both of whom were home for a brief visit between tours of Italy. She gathered the two had been traveling together for several years, spending far more time abroad than in their native land. The daughter was scandalously tan, especially against the pale ivory skirt and black bodice of her gown. Her name was Imogen, and Anne suspected she was rather fast. "I always forget how cold it gets in London," she said with a shiver.

"At least it's warmer than Weymouth," Anne replied. "The winds from the sea go right through a body."

Imogen clucked. "You should make Simon take you on honeymoon to Sicily. Or Athens, or Crete—anywhere in Greece, really. I've never made it past the Adriatic myself. It may be time to convince my mother to range farther afield." Her smile turned sly. "But she's so fond of Italian men, and I am not sure she'll find Greek ones to be a suitable replacement." Anne blushed and her new cousin laughed. "That's better—you were far too pale for a bride on her wedding day," she said. Her gray eyes were different from Simon's. They glittered like sixpences, bright and hard. "Do you love him?" she asked.

Anne was taken aback but refused to be cowed. "I think I shall, in time. There is much to love about him."

Imogen shook her head. "That is precisely what he would have said." She glanced at Simon, who was conversing affably with Anne's father while Mrs. Pym beamed happily from beneath a riotously feathered headpiece. "You will have the most pragmatic children in the world. Promise me you will set them to solving serious problems—the Irish Question, the electoral system, abolition of slavery."

"I shall read them Pitt's speeches as bedtime tales," Anne said archly.

Imogen's lips quirked. "Well, at least they will sleep soundly." She took a sip of her coffee, to which she'd added neither cream nor sugar. "Where *are* you honeymooning?"

"We aren't," Anne confessed. "London is quite exotic enough for me." Also, though she wasn't about to admit this to Imogen, now that her own future was secure she wanted to waste no time in arranging Evangeline's marriage. The Season would be ending after summer and they could honeymoon then, if Simon felt the need.

At length the food was taken away, the guests made their farewells and the new bride and groom departed for home in a coach with the Underwood coat of arms. Anne was surprised to find herself exhausted, considering she had done nothing more strenuous than sit in a room and talk to people. Simon tucked her gloved hand into his elbow, his brow furrowing in concern. "Would you prefer to postpone the wedding night?"

She smiled at his courtesy and at the warmth of his arm beneath her palm, but shook her head. "I promise to be only a little skittish," she replied. "Hecuba has given me a general sketch of the proceedings. Not an actual drawing," she amended as he gaped. "Just more of the specifics than my mother offered. She was trying so hard to be delicate that I only understood one thought in ten."

Simon smiled. "Well, the mystery will be solved soon enough."

After dinner he gave her an hour to undress before he came through the connecting door. Her bedroom was a cozy room decorated in rich burgundy with green vine accents on the curtains and counterpane. The act itself was a trifle awkward but not unpleasant, and when Simon had kissed her goodnight and trundled back into his own room, Anne lay back beneath the covers and was soon asleep.

She took tea and toast in her private parlor the next morning—an indulgence she planned to make shamelessly frequent—and read with satisfaction the marriage announcement in the paper. *Miss Anne Pym, to the Right Honorable the Earl of Underwood...*

It was a very promising beginning.

CHAPTER 2

The first invitation arrived later that same afternoon. Anne savored the contrast of black ink on creamy paper, and let her fingers briefly trace the elegant hand, looping and slender and scrolled. The event itself was a small dinner given by Lord and Lady Heatherton. They had always been quite warm to the family Pym, so Anne was not surprised they were the first to reach out now that she was respectable again.

At the dinner, she was delighted to find that Mr. Bertram Egley was also present, and she managed to secure a promise for him to come by for tea the following Wednesday. Anne plotted to invite Evangeline as well, and see if that particular flame could be easily relit.

But alas, the rest of the party were not nearly as warm, as she found when she tried to talk to the gentleman seated on her left. "Are you enjoying the Season this year, Lord Asherton?" A rather obvious opening gambit, but Anne was out of practice with genteel conversation. At least it had the virtue of being polite, if disgracefully dull.

His lordship's large brown eyes rolled her way, considering her question. "Quite." Satisfied with this monosyllable, his lordship sawed off another portion of partridge and happily resumed chewing.

Anne paused.

His lordship chewed.

It seemed that was all she would get for a response. She cast a glance at Simon, but he and Lord Heatherton were deeply involved in talk of horses and bloodlines. There would be no help from that quarter. She waited until Lord Asherton swallowed, then tried again. "I thought yesterday's weather was particularly fine."

"Mmm," was all his lordship offered. He reached for his glass and took a prolonged draught of wine.

From somewhere down the table, Anne heard someone titter. This was becoming embarrassing. Desperately, she turned to Viscount Clary, who was seated on her right. "And you, my lord? Are you enjoying London?"

He arched one pale brow at her. "One doesn't enjoy London, Lady Underwood: one endures it."

Mrs. Audley, on the viscount's other side, laughed approvingly. "How true, my lord, how true. There are so many people, and so few of them are worth the effort of meeting." Her gaze brushed Anne's and then moved on, so quickly that Anne wasn't entirely certain she'd really heard the insult.

No, she admitted to herself, that wasn't true. She'd heard it quite clearly. The poison had been subtly but unmistakably applied.

Across the table, Bertram Egley spoke up. "I am always delighted to see new faces in town," he said.

"You would be," Viscount Clary said. Mr. Egley blinked and looked puzzled, even as the viscount's smile stretched like a snake on a sun-warmed rock. "I know you pride yourself on your talent for tasting food, Mr. Egley. Is our hostess's table up to your high standards?"

He'd pitched his tone perfectly—two seats away, at the foot of the table, Lady Heatherton heard him and stiffened.

The shot passed right over Mr. Egley's head. "Oh, the curried partridge is excellent," he said, eager as always to discuss his favorite subject. "Though I would have added a touch more saffron and a bit less salt, for preference..." He continued in this vein, waxing particularly eloquent on the less than desirable fish course, while the viscount mimed attention and Mrs. Audley smothered her amusement behind the lip of her wineglass.

A lady across the table—Anne thought her name was Mrs. Bell —flicked a glance at poor Lady Heatherton, who was visibly beginning to wilt. "We are fortunate to have someone so thoughtful with us tonight, Mr. Egley," she said. "I'm sure Lady Heatherton never thought to excite so much comment with her menu."

"Did she not?" Mr. Egley sounded sincerely surprised and turned to face the hostess. "She ought to have—you have clearly taken much care about the courses and their harmony with one another, my lady. It shows a creative culinary turn of mind, which is all too rare even in so large a place as London." He bowed in homage, and Lady Heatherton blushed with pleasure.

"And you, Lady Underwood?" Mrs. Audley continued, her voice laudanum-sweet. "Do you find the meal as impressive as our connoisseur does?"

All eyes fixed on Anne, who had just taken a bite of the infamous partridge.

She swallowed as hastily as was polite. "I find everything rather dazzling," she admitted. It was true enough, and none of the other replies her mind was offering her could be spoken aloud in company. *I find the best seasoning for a meal is kindness and generosity, Mrs. Audley.* Or: *Perhaps, Lord Clary, I am not yet jaded or indolent enough to be bored in the middle of one of the world's greatest cities.*

"Where are you from, my lady?" that oily gentleman asked.

She pasted a smile on her face. "My family lives in Dorset, my lord—though we have been in the city now for the better part of a year."

"So we have heard," Mrs. Audley murmured with a bland smile. Anne had nothing to say to this, but the lady spared her and continued smoothly, "Still, I can see how the color and glitter of London society could be blinding for someone used to a more muted palette."

Her glance took in Anne's cream-colored frock with lace that had once been bright gold but was now closer to mustard.

Anne lowered her eyes to her plate and let the conversation move on without her.

When the Pyms had come down from Dorset last Season, both Anne and Evangeline had been outfitted with new wardrobes. All decisions about color, style and form, however, had been filtered through the prism of Mrs. Pym's taste. Now Anne was brutally reminded how her mother's sensibilities were mired in the narrow columnlike silhouettes and fitted sleeves of past decades. The more *à la mode* ladies of the *ton* currently flaunted gowns with heavy skirts that belled out from a tightly corseted waist. The sleeves of Mrs. Audley's shell-pink satin gown, very stylish, extended past her shoulders like the wings of fat baby angels in Italian paintings.

As she swallowed the last bite of partridge, Anne decided it was time to put her new status and wealth to good use. For once she had both the money and the autonomy she needed to clothe herself as she wished.

She felt a rebellious inclination to be dramatic about it.

The next morning, the new Countess of Underwood descended upon the modiste and ordered a round dozen gowns. She chose rich velvets, bright prints, shining silks and lush brocades—not a pale pastel to be seen. Metallics and lace details and complex pleating and draping were everywhere, with shawls and gloves and underthings to match. Three half-finished dresses were close enough to her measurements that the modiste promised to complete them at once and send them over the following day. Anne felt drunk on color and texture, and especially on the ability to finally say for herself what she wanted and what she rejected. The slight twinge of guilt that thrummed in the back of her mind at the thought of the unwonted expense was merely a spice to her excitement.

～

The earl had just lifted a glass of burgundy when his wife walked in for dinner. The countess had time to glide calmly across the room, take a seat in the chair the footman pulled out for her and murmur a gentle word of thanks before Simon realized he was frozen, glass extended, just watching her from his seat across the table.

Her dress was as red as the wine.

He took a hasty sip to clear a mouth gone suddenly dry, but still he stared as the footmen began serving courses. The gown was new—it had to be new—he surely would have remembered seeing her in it before. It was a velvet something-or-other, low on the shoulder and puffed in the sleeves, with a long, curving neckline set off by a single golden brooch. The rich color suited her, but more than that it was clear that she loved this gown and she loved moving in it. There was a relish in every gesture that he'd never seen before, and it was slowly but steadily unmaking him. The lift of a shoulder, the gesture of an arm, the angle of her body as she leaned slightly forward over her food. When she took a spoonful of soup and idly licked an errant drop from her lips, Simon nearly groaned aloud.

His bride was absurdly fuckable.

How on earth had he never seen it before?

It was an appalling realization. They had been getting on quite well, in Simon's opinion—pleasant companionship, quiet unity, a general sense of mutual approbation and warmth. It was a relief to have someone managing the household affairs so Simon could deal with the financial burdens of the estate, not to mention the country properties and a few speculative deals he'd been dabbling in. And every night, before retiring to separate rooms, they shared a few minutes of necessary marital relations in the interest of creating an heir.

And now this peaceful calm was shattered. Simon knew he had a lustful side, the same as any man, but it had never felt so monstrous and tigerish as it did now. Her waist looked slimmer— she must have had her maid pull her corset more snug than usual. Was that restrictive undergarment the same lush red, over the pure white of her chemise? What must that velvet sleeve feel like against her skin, in the tender crook of her elbow? How slowly could he pull that low neckline down to expose a breast for tasting? He shivered, imagining the rustling sound he would surely hear if he hiked up all those skirts and petticoats to get to the woman beneath. She would be warm, with all that bulky fabric— warm and rosy and soft beneath his hands. Sweet beneath his mouth.

It was impossible to eat in this condition, but it was equally impossible for him to rise and leave the table. For one thing it would be rude, and he felt rude enough as it was. For another...

Well, for another, he was so damn hard he wasn't sure he was physically capable of standing up. Any attempt was liable to leave him keeled over on the floor, grinding his cock into the Aubusson for relief, raving and clutching at the weave with desperate hands. But even that horrid prospect would be preferable to what would happen if he laid hands on Anne herself—in his current state he couldn't help but be rough, and she would react with all the horror and fear such viciousness deserved.

A gently bred bride deserved better than a beast. He needed to get himself under control.

He forced himself to focus on the conversation. It helped to keep his eyes on his plate. "I've had a letter from Hecuba," Anne was saying. "She mentions she and John are expecting. July, they think."

Simon addressed his reply to the breast of pheasant before him. "That's wonderful news."

"There are some warnings from the doctor that have John in

quite a state," Anne went on, "but Hecuba herself scorns the risks."

Hecuba would, of course. She was bolder by far than either of her cousins. Simon shied away from thoughts of John, to whom he hadn't written since he and his new bride had left town and set up that paint shop of theirs. Almost a year ago now, but the wound was still fresh. He thoughtlessly lifted his eyes, caught a flash of his wife's curving shoulder and hastily resumed poking at a potato. "It will be good to have an extra link in the chain of succession," he murmured.

"Until we have a child of our own." Anne's smile was full of such hesitant hopefulness that Simon's heart nearly broke with it. He lifted his lips in return, but he couldn't vouch for the integrity of the expression. Anne seemed satisfied, however, and proceeded to apprise him on the reception of his brother's latest painting, which had been unveiled to great acclaim by those in the know. Simon managed to make it through the subsequent courses, until his wife left the room and he hurled his restless body into a chair with a cigar and a stiff brandy.

The easy, placid marriage he'd built for himself had vanished. All because he'd never thought to imagine his wife wearing red.

In the countess's bedroom Anne waited and waited, but the usual hour for Simon's visit passed and the connecting door stayed shut. It was a puzzle. Eventually she grew tired of turning it over unprofitably in her head. Her slippered feet made no noise on the carpet, and the well-oiled hinges barely breathed as she opened the door that linked the earl's bedroom to hers.

She stopped, transfixed by what she saw.

Simon was there, one arm resting on the mantelpiece, his body bent as if in pain. He had removed his jacket, and below his waist his clothing had been peeled back as if some nighttime flower had been caught mid-bloom. His eyes were screwed shut, his face twisted, and his other hand was working hard at something between his legs...

Anne caught her breath. He was pleasuring himself.

The part of him he'd wrapped his right hand around was the same part he used in her. But with her his motions were always gentle and moderate, punctuated occasionally by a muffled gasp at the end. Now, though, he moved as if punishing himself, each breath bursting out of him, every muscle knotted with effort.

Anne licked her lips. She could only see glimpses between the furious motion of his strokes, hints of skin and hair and shadow in the constantly changing light of the fire in the hearth. She wanted to see more. It was brutal and vulgar and almost certainly immoral, but right now she needed to watch him almost as badly as she needed to draw her next breath.

A groan was wrung from him, and Anne ducked back slightly into the doorway, where the shadows would hide her should he chance to open his eyes. His hand jerked once, twice more, then he erupted, long ropes of white jetting out of him and into the chamber pot below. He'd known this would happen, she realized. The pot was there because he'd anticipated this.

Anne didn't know what to make of that. She felt restless, angry in some indefinable way. Her skin was all at once too big—or too small—her legs unsteady, her heart racing unevenly in her breast.

Simon sighed, a long, dark sound that slid against her bones, painful and profound. Anne stepped back into her room and silently closed the door.

She gave herself a moment just to breathe, trying to cool the flush she felt in her cheeks, then lifted her hand and knocked. "Simon?" she called, her voice rougher than she expected. She coughed a little to clear her throat.

After a moment the door opened. Her husband stood there, slightly ruddy, eyes bright, his clothing restored to its natural order. The pulse at the base of his throat was fluttering, betraying him despite the show of calm. "My apologies," he said. "I find I'm feeling a little out of sorts tonight. I think it's best if I simply keep to my own bed."

Anne stared at that telltale patch of pulsing skin. She was alarmingly tempted to reach out and press her hand to his chest, to feel how his heart beat there. It struck her that she'd never really touched him, never slid her hand along his skin just for the feel of it. They'd never even really looked at each other, not without at least three layers of nightclothes and blankets and the comforting distance of the uncandled night.

It was what she had expected—but suddenly it was no longer enough. "Is there anything I can do?" she asked.

He smiled, as coolly proper as if it were their wedding day again and the vicar were standing between them with his prayer-book. "I'm sure I shall be well again tomorrow by the time of the Morleys' ball," he said. "Until tomorrow, my dear." His slight bow was still decorous, but Anne marked the precise moment when his eyes strayed to her bosom beneath the fine lawn of her nightdress. A flare of heat warmed his eyes, then he turned and shut the door.

Anne was left breathless and stunned. He'd never looked at her that way before—not when they'd met, not when they'd married and not afterward. Nobody else ever had either. She had assumed that it was simply not the kind of feeling she could inspire in another person. She had put this dispiriting thought aside to pine over in the privacy of the night, and focused on more achievable ambitions: marriage, respectability, and eventually a family of her own.

But she had achieved those goals now, or would soon enough. She'd been wondering what she was going to do with her time until she had children to fill it. She'd been wondering what else there was for her to want.

Well now she knew.

That darkness, that desperation, that terrifying ecstasy that had gripped her usually steady husband—she wanted that.

She wanted him.

She could guess the name of this feeling that pulsed within her. It was lust, primal and simple and strong. She'd felt echoes of it before, but never had it seemed to stretch out to occupy every atom of her being like this. Before, she'd always ignored it—and she had been ignored in return by the distant, unattainable objects of that lust.

No more. She was a countess now, after all, not a penniless miss. A countess had a chance of getting what she wanted.

15

If she was only brave enough to reach for it.

CHAPTER 3

*S*imon had his valet Tully retie his cravat three times before he found it stiff enough to satisfy. He needed the security of a perfectly pressed and folded piece of pure white linen. He needed the tightness around his neck, holding his head up and reminding him that he was a gentleman rather than an animal. He picked a dark frock coat that nipped in at the waist and a deep blue waistcoat beneath that. Cool colors, calm hues. Restraint would be his watchword, even if it killed him.

He was waiting at the door when his countess appeared at the top of the stairs.

Tonight she was wearing gold.

The fabric shimmered with every movement as she descended the stairs. The skirts were wide but the bodice was tight, the shoulders narrower than those worn by women on the daring edge of fashion. As she grew closer, he saw that the gold on her shoulders and bosom had been artfully pleated and folded, a gift begging to be unwrapped, layer upon layer of edges drawing the eye with sharp, geometric lines that contrasted with the sweet curves of neck and shoulder and breast. And above that bodice only bare skin, set off by a doubled strand of pearls around her neck, which matched the cool ivory of her long gloves. This was not the sudden carnal shock of the red dress—this pull was something more fragile, more mysterious, though just as alluring for being subtle.

He wondered what she would do if he dropped to his knees in worship.

Perhaps this transformation was simply the natural result of fortune, of not being compelled to limit her tastes to the cheaper fabrics or the less expensive dressmakers and seamstresses. If so, Simon was responsible for his own torture, as he'd explicitly told Anne she could draw on his funds as much as she liked. He imagined this particular gown had been very dear, but quite honestly even if she told him the whole thing was woven from real and solid gold he would consider it worth the price.

She was breathtaking.

He bowed wordlessly and extended an arm. Anne accepted it gracefully, and together they went to meet the coach.

The darkness of the coach's interior was both a blessing and a torment. The window's open curtains let in a constantly sliding square of yellow light from the gas lamps that lined the streets. The clip of the horses' hooves echoed oddly around the city's turnings, and for one disoriented moment Simon felt as though the team and driver were outpacing them, leaving him and Anne behind in the darkness, faced with each other. "The pearls are lovely," he commented. "They suit you very well."

Her ivory gloves gleamed as she lifted her fingers to touch the necklace. Simon's eyes were riveted to the movement. "A wedding gift from your cousin Imogen," she said. Then, to his amazement, she leaned forward so the light fell across her neck and the swell of her breasts.

Simon's gaze flicked up in surprise, just in time to catch the small hope that went rushing across her face before she smoothed it out into placidity once more. Her fingers stayed on her neck, the paleness of her glove pulling at his attention and drawing his eye deliberately toward her décolletage.

Good God—his wife was trying to seduce him.

He'd never expected this to happen. All his life, Simon had divided the world of women into two categories: "proper" being one and "seducing or seducible" being the other. He didn't quite know when or why this had happened, but the subcategory of "wife" and more specifically "my future wife" had always been filed under "proper." Perhaps it was something to do with the title or the lineage or the need to produce an heir—a wife of noble blood was a required acquisition for an earl, as priggish and unexciting as a paragraph in Debrett's.

Simon was not, however, a man to cling to a thought just for the sake of stubbornness, not when there was evidence that he'd been terribly blind and unforgivably wrong. For right in front of him was Anne, her breath lifting what really was a marvelous bosom—*how* had he possibly overlooked her bosom? he should put out his eyes for that sin, except that without eyes he could no longer appreciate the aforementioned bosom—and so beautifully, achingly poised, with just a hint of yearning in her eyes...

The earl leaned forward and placed his fingertips against the back of her ivory glove. Anne went still, breath caught in surprise, eyes going wide as the streetlight's beam swept across her face and away again. "Very lovely," Simon murmured—then, feeling strangely bold, he moved his fingertips down. Glove slid against glove as his fingers trailed down the outside of her wrist, then deliberately to the upper swell of a breast, hooking slightly beneath the gleaming fabric of that bodice.

At the touch of his gloved fingers against her bare skin, Anne let out a sigh. It was a small sound, barely audible, and if Simon had not been leaning so attentively forward he would never have caught it. But small though it was, it was laced with an undeniable sense of pure physical pleasure.

He'd never heard his wife make such a sound before.

And hard upon that thought came another, more sobering: his wife had never been pleasured before.

Or if she had, he'd not been the man to do it.

Simon didn't know which prospect appalled him more—the

thought that either Anne had never had her body's needs teased and tempted and satisfied, or the thought that she knew how it felt when desire set spur to the pulse and raced beneath the skin, and that she'd been waiting for him to manfully take charge and put those cravings to their natural use. No, he realized, that wasn't right—surely Anne was frank enough that if there were something she wanted from him, she would ask.

But then...she *was* asking. Not bluntly, perhaps, but she was a lady and had been raised with a different rulebook of correct behavior. She could invite, entrance and entice, but it might take a great deal of courage for her to speak her mind on this, of all topics.

Simon found he disliked the idea of forcing Anne to be that brave. It felt...uneven. As though he were treating his wife like a child, deciding what was best for her, coaxing her forward as though she were a toddler and he a knowing parent. Nothing of what he felt in this moment came anywhere near the word *parental*.

"This is going to be a very difficult night," he said, half smiling at his own unease.

"Is it?" The teasing lilt in her voice made him shiver even as his fingers stayed warm and solid on the slope of her breast. "Are Lord and Lady Morley so stern?" she murmured.

"Not at all." He moved his fingers just slightly, just enough that she could feel the friction, that she couldn't forget he was touching her. "Nor are their guests likely to prove troublesome. It is simply that..." He stroked her again, a one-inch caress. She pulled in a deep, much-delayed breath and her breast swelled deliciously beneath Simon's fingers. "I cannot ravish you now, not without leaving you disheveled, and you have taken such care to look perfectly glorious. But if I wait to ravish you later, I must wait several hours to do so, and my patience is likely to be very tested."

"And what of my patience?" Anne returned. Her tone struck sparks from him like flint against steel. She licked her lips and fixed him with a keen gaze. "You could have kept your intentions to yourself and left me to enjoy the evening in peace. Instead you offer me the promise of ravishment, and I shall be as tormented as you by the hours spent waiting."

"Will you?" Simon breathed. "Do you know how it feels to desire someone, Anne? How it builds low, like a fire in the belly? How it aches deep in the bones?" He turned his hand and cupped her breast—boldly, fully, the touch warming him even through all those layers of fabric. "Do you know about need?"

"I do." Was that her nipple, hardening against his palm? Simon's mouth went dry. Meanwhile Anne swallowed hard, looked up at him and said very clearly, "And I know how it feels when that need is satisfied."

It was Simon's turn to go hard. Breath hissed out between his clenched teeth as he fought to keep from putting his hands on every blessed, tempting inch of her.

At that very moment, the coach lurched to a halt. Simon and Anne would have collided had he not automatically caught her by the arms. "This is as near as I can come, my lord," the driver called down.

"Thank you, Ben." Simon sucked in a long breath and willed himself back to a semblance of respectable gentility. Anne was still looking up at him, flushed even in the dimness, eyes bright and lips slightly parted. His thumbs stroked down her skin once more before he dropped his hands. "I must remember to ask you more about that statement later," he promised, then Ben was opening the coach door and it was time to reenter the larger, colder world.

They had arrived a little way down the street from Lord and Lady Morley's home, which was besieged by stopped vehicles disgorging their guests in the direction of the well-lit doorway. Anne was grateful that the short walk gave her time to regain her presence of mind, otherwise she feared disgracing herself before their host and hostess.

Ravished, he'd said—as if he meant it, as if he were looking forward to it. The word had lingered in the space between them, making her almost painfully conscious of the softly insistent pressure of his gloved fingers against her skin while her heart pounded beneath. The satisfaction when he'd cupped her fully, and the rush of increased hunger that had followed. She'd recognized the symptoms easily enough, though Simon himself had never stirred her so before. Could it really be only the gowns that had changed things between them? Her hand on Simon's arm tightened, feeling the movement of muscle beneath the gentlemanly cloth of coat and shirt. She remembered the folds of linen, white in the firelight, tumbled around his waist...

Anne broke off that particular thought, which would not bear polite and public scrutiny. She would have to be proper and correct for a while before she indulged herself and her husband.

They entered the ball and Simon introduced her to Lord and Lady Morley. The former had a shocking swoop of white hair and the latter was as wrinkly and warm and plump as a Christmas raisin. No hint of anything lecherous or louche could possibly come within ten feet of such a decorous pair, and Anne pushed her hedonistic musings aside and tried to concentrate on conversation.

The guests tonight were all very good *ton*, too elevated for her own family to be present. The golden gown, which she'd thought just a hair too ostentatious in the comfort of her room, turned out to be outmatched by countless other dresses of tissue, silk and satin, often brocaded and embroidered and bejeweled. Had some women not been considerately dressed in velvets and chiffons that collected and held the light, the entire company might have perished from refraction.

As they moved through the room, Anne became grateful for her husband's solid presence, like an anchor bracing her against the wash and ebb of the murmuring crowd. Occasionally his fingers brushed the back of her upper arm or the small of her back, and that slight touch brought a blush to heat the planes of her cheeks. He chuckled low and lush at some lord's witticism, and the sound curled lazily at the base of her spine. He bowed to a new acquaintance, raising the lady's hand almost—but not quite —to his lips, and Anne watched the quiet grace of his movements and wondered that the lady could look so cool and reserved at the touch.

By the time he turned and asked her to dance, she had half forgotten her goal to earn society's unreserved respect and admiration. On the outside Anne remained poised and pleasant, but on the inside she was a seething, sizzling, riotous mass of nerves and blood and a heart that couldn't seem to keep a steady rhythm.

How on earth would she keep up the charade?

She let Simon's strong arms guide her through the steps of the waltz. He nodded at another couple as they passed, and in a quiet, conversational tone he asked, "Did you have someone else? Another suitor?" He paused before going on. "Another man?"

The meaning was obvious and thoroughly shocking. Anne went stiff, might even have stumbled if he hadn't been there to catch her. She couldn't believe he'd asked such a question in the middle of the Morley's ball. Nor did she think he'd asked out of jealousy—his expression was cool and unconcerned, though he was slightly flushed. Nothing that could not be explained by the exertion of the dance. Well, if he wanted to be daring, she could play along. "What if I had?" she asked defiantly.

His hand on hers tightened briefly. Then, "*Had*," he said. "Past tense." His smile flashed at her, stealing her breath. "That's all I need to know—though I'll listen if there's more you want to tell me."

Some of the tension went out of her shoulders. "I shouldn't joke," she said, blushing. "Not now—not about this. There was never such a man. I was a maiden when we wed." The next part of her admission was harder to get out. She licked her lips and dredged up a gracious smile for a passing duke and his duchess, who inclined her feather-decked head in acknowledgement. "The only pleasure I've known I've obtained at my own hands."

He caught his breath—she heard it catch and felt his shoulders loosen beneath her hands as he let that breath out, slowly. "That...was very improper of you." His luxurious tone eliminated all rebuke from the statement. "May I ask: was it a habit or only a momentary adventure?"

She arched her eyebrows at him, every inch the dignified countess despite the fact that they were discussing self-pleasure in the middle of an open dance floor. "I would describe it as something like a stolen pastry—sweet, furtive and about as frequently enjoyed." He laughed aloud, turning heads in their direction. Anne gave the onlookers her most demure smile until she and Simon spun out of sight behind the other waltzing couples. Traces of amusement still hung on his lips when she looked back at him. "I suppose I don't have to tell you that women have carnal lusts just as men do."

Her husband sighed, that lingering smile vanishing. "Idiotically, I hadn't realized this fundamental truth until very recently. That is to say...I had been thinking of a wife's needs in a very limited, decorous sense. Not with any real depth or consideration." His dark eyes regarded her, still and solemn.

Anne glanced away, feeling as though they were drifting into murkier waters. "I have been making the same mistake about husbands that you have made about wives," she said. His thumb came to rest in her palm, warm and soothing like an ember on the hearth. The heat made her brave again, steel in her spine. "You have had mistresses or affairs, I presume?"

"Had," Simon said quietly. "Past tense."

Anne's heart unknotted a little in relief. She had hoped for at least a little fidelity in these important early years. But the license his sex gave him for—she groped for a word—for *licentiousness*—could prove to be advantageous at present. "Then you have a great deal more experience in these matters than I do."

Simon shrugged, one shoulder rising and falling beneath her gloved hand. "Experience only goes so far. Some years ago I knew a *demimondaine*—an opera singer, all black hair and throaty voice. She loved red roses, the darker the better. My last mistress, however, was inexplicably fond of lilies. It's a facile example, I admit, but a vital fact—every woman is unique and particular." Another pair of dancers swung past, burgundy and blue, and Simon pulled Anne close to prevent collision. He bent, his lips nearly brushing her ear. "And the fact is: I have not had much experience with you, Anne."

It was oddly comforting, the thought that this was something new for both of them. She would not be alone in this. Anne looked into Simon's dark eyes and whispered, "Not yet."

He made a sound low in his throat, a wordless throb of surprise and pleasure and curiosity. The music swirled to an end and the dancers drifted away. Simon held out his arm, a glint in his dark eyes.

It was time.

A footman was dispatched to ready the coach while they bade farewell to their hosts. Simon helped her up the small step, his hand sturdy beneath her trembling fingers. He leaped in after her, rapped on the roof and drew the curtains shut.

In the sudden darkness, Anne nearly lost her nerve. Her hands were clenched tightly in her lap. She was on the point of opening her mouth to say something— anything—when she felt Simon's large hands cover hers.

Her fingers tensed in surprise, then relaxed. He was so warm. Slowly, his hands slid upward: along the backs of her gloved hands, lingering on the tender skin of her upper arms, traversing the high curve of shoulder that the bodice of her gown left bare. They rested there, strangely heavy, and Anne realized suddenly that Simon had taken off his gloves. One hand—his left—moved upward, following the line of her jaw and resting gentle fingertips on the slope of her cheekbone. Anne leaned in to the caress, seeking more of his warmth, more of his skin against hers. As his palm curved to cup her cheek, there was movement in the darkness.

Simon kissed her.

They'd kissed before, a handful of times—delicate, almost chaste touches of the lips. This was another species of kiss entirely. Dark and addictive, unbearably sweet, occasionally messy when the coach turned a corner and his mouth slid slightly askew against hers. The slight scrape from the brush of his trimmed moustache against her sensitive lips, a contrast that rattled her somewhere deep inside. There were sounds, too—gasps, small moans, and wet sounds. Tongues were apparently involved in this kind of kiss, which Anne would have found repulsive if she'd been told about it beforehand, but it didn't *feel* repulsive. It felt...decadent. Delicious. Depraved, even.

When the coach finally came to a halt, they broke apart and Simon twitched the curtains open again. Anne was shocked to find her hands had done fatal damage to her husband's cravat. "I'm sorry," she said automatically, trying to pat the linen back into place.

"So am I," he chuckled and tugged on a lock of her hair, which she belatedly realized was in a similar state of catastrophe. She blushed fiercely and managed to avert her eyes from Simon, from Ben, from the butler who opened the front door and the footman who took Simon's gloves and hat. She might have made it all the way upstairs unlooked-at had her husband not stopped her in the foyer. "Anne," he said gently, "you realize you have nothing to be ashamed of?"

She blinked. It sounded so easy when he said it. As though she had not spent the entire evening trying to mask her thoughts and desires from the outside world. As though she had not spent *years* trying to pretend there was nothing improper in the darkness behind her eyes, nothing riotous or risky in her heart, beating at the walls of good behavior and threatening to knock etiquette to the floor and bloody its nose.

She looked at Phillips, the butler. He had those red spots in his cheeks again, but unless she was mistaken...yes. He was smiling. Just barely, but the evidence was there.

How clearly Anne remembered his blustering disapproval when she'd visited the house before. Yet there he was, the edges of his thin lips tilted decidedly upward. All his earlier snobbishness had melted away like snow in summer, simply because she had changed her name and decorated it with a title. He'd never even thought to question her orders in this house—a fact she had, until this moment, not really considered.

Anne let herself bask in the realization. Everything was vastly, wonderfully different now. She was married. A countess. She had a title and a fortune. The old rigid rules had, overnight, become guidelines.

She felt a sudden, violent need to celebrate her freedom. She wanted to curse. She wanted to dance naked in the moonlight. She wanted to hurl a glass of brandy into a blazing fireplace and roar like a pirate in a torrid novel.

She wanted ravishment—and she didn't care whose.

"My lord," she said with all a countess's innate dignity, "I think you ought to take me to bed."

"My lady," Simon replied, "it would be my pleasure."

a fire had been laid in the earl's bedchamber. Simon lit a branch of candles at the hearth while Anne stripped off her gloves and kicked her slippers to one side. She clenched her stockinged toes against the carpet, the lushness of the pile easing some of her anxiety. She felt as though she stood at the base of some great mountain—there was something at the peak she wanted very much, but the climb was daunting and arduous. Her hands wanted to tremble, no matter how bold she felt. "This is rather awkward," she said.

"It is," her husband agreed. He set the candles on a side table and turned to face her. "How should we begin?"

Anne frowned. "Shouldn't you know? Surely you're better suited to guide me than the reverse."

"If you like," he said pleasantly. "I'm not sure there are many rules for this sort of thing."

Anne had had enough of rules. She raised her chin. "If there are, let's ignore them."

Simon smiled. "Let's." He put one shoulder back, then the other, sliding free of his tailored coat and letting it drop over the back of a nearby chair. In the candlelight his shirtsleeves glowed ivory, pale and luminous. Anne expected him to reach for his cravat next, but instead he crossed the room and stopped in front of her. "You might be more comfortable without the pins in your hair," he suggested.

She swallowed, nodded and turned her back to him. On the dark wood of the bedroom door their shadows mingled—his tall and broad in the shoulder, hers belling out wide below. She watched his shadow-hands lift and felt his real fingers in her hair, pulling each lock and curl free with gentle precision. "Hold out your hand," he said, and when she complied he began letting the pins fall into her palm, a slowly accumulating pile of metal. Each pin started off cold, but soon warmed to match the heat coming off her skin. It was surprisingly difficult to stand still during all this, hand held up, waiting while he sought each individual pin in the dark sweep of her hair. Her arm tensed and tightened, almost to the point of pain. She couldn't seem to remember how to breathe noiselessly, and the sound was harsh in her own ears.

And then he bent and kissed the side of her neck. Just the touch of his mouth, with the warm lips and the rough bristle of his mustache, and Anne decided she'd been patient enough. She'd been patient for *years*.

She let the hairpins fall to the carpet and turned to face her husband. His cravat was already a ruin, so she had no qualms about twining her left hand in it and pulling his head down to hers. It didn't take much force, as he seemed eager enough to comply.

For the first time, Anne kissed him.

He let her set the pace, which pleased her so much she pushed forward, the kiss hungry and brutal. She used every trick and method he'd shown her on the drive home, making up a few of her own, letting intuition and inclination guide her. Long, hard drugging strokes of the tongue. Mouths open, devouring. All while her right hand was busy undoing the buttons on his waistcoat, tugging his shirt from his waistline, then sliding blissfully onto the skin of his stomach and sides.

He pulled his mouth from hers and hissed with startled pleasure.

Anne put her face against his chest, finding it easier to feel him rather than to look. For now. As he breathed, she let her right hand wander, let her palm slide up the solid flesh beneath the linen, let her fingers tangle in the thicket of hair on his chest. Simon shrugged out of the waistcoat—oh, what a shift in the muscle that made, dancing beneath her palm—and went to work on his trousers, surely undoing the buttons with more finesse than Anne would have had. She let him struggle and then, when the dark wool fell away from his hips, she took her left hand and pushed it through the folds of fabric to cup the hard, ready length of him.

The skin there felt surprisingly delicate, almost fragile—not so his fingers, which banded tight on her arms as she grasped him. His breath surged in and out of his chest, broad muscle heaving beneath her touch. Anne stroked her left hand slowly up and down, curling her fingers around his girth, learning the shape of him in a way all their well-mannered nights together had failed to teach her. "I saw you do this," she murmured.

He went still and so did she. She hadn't meant to admit to that. He throbbed a little against her fingers while she stared at the base of his throat. His pulse was fluttering again. Her heart matched time.

"When?" he murmured.

There was just enough heat in the question to thaw her frozen voice. "The other night," she said. "When you didn't come to my chamber, I opened the door. And—saw you. Watched you." She began stroking him again, her courage rising to meet her desire. Without conscious guidance, her voice turned low and smoky. "You looked...desperate."

"I felt desperate," he groaned. "You were wearing red."

"So you like me in red?" She sped up her strokes.

His fingers on her arms spasmed briefly at the increased pace. His breath was coming in quick pants now. "I liked that you liked it," he gasped. "The dress. The fabric. I could tell. You looked—so pleased. Pleasured. Decadent. Oh, god." He reached down and grasped her wrist, preventing her from moving. "If you don't stop, this will all be over very quickly." His head was bent, his eyes clamped shut with effort.

Anne leaned ever so slightly forward and closed the distance between them, her lips at his ear. "And what if I don't want to stop?"

"Then I'm going to come," Simon moaned.

She hadn't heard the term before but could guess what it meant. "Not here, you aren't," she said firmly. "I may not be terribly experienced, but even I know that's no way to get an heir." His grip on her wrist was nearly painful now, his hands shaking a little, his chest quaking beneath her palm. Anne realized she liked seeing him like this. "Release my hand."

He did, instantly. The sudden relief from the pressure on her wrist ran up her arm and arrived in her throat as a rush of unexpected triumph. He'd obeyed her command without a second of hesitation.

She found she liked that even more.

The hand that was on his chest glided up to his throat. A gentle pull on one end of the linen and his cravat came loose. Simon stayed still, trembling like a hound on the scent, waiting to see what she would ask of him next.

Slowly, she wrapped the soft linen around the hard length between his legs.

Thus guarded, her left hand began to stroke again. Slowly but firmly, learning what rhythm he responded to, listening to the soft, keening sounds he made when she swept a thumb across the crown of him beneath the fabric. His voice grew higher and higher in pitch as she moved her hand faster and faster. She wanted him as desperate as he'd been before—wanted to feel his climax in her hands rather than watching from across the room. He was shaking, and from that she knew he was close. She pressed her lips to his temple, tasting the salt and sweat on his skin. "Don't you dare come," she whispered.

He spilled at once, as she'd secretly hoped he would. Victory filled her up like wine, rich and sweet and heady. Here was a man —tall, sturdy, titled, respected and strong— and he had all but fallen to pieces at a simple touch of her hand.

It made her wonder what the rest of her body could do.

"Anne..." he murmured, his face turning into the curve of her neck. "I'm so sorry..."

"Don't be," she replied. She kissed him one more time and wiped the remains of his seed from her hands with the end of his now definitely ruined cravat. Gleefully, she tossed it into the fire, a sacrifice to her older, colder life. After a long moment, she felt him come up behind her and move her hair aside. Within moments he had the buttons of her gown worked free—she stepped out of the heavy garment and laid it aside on the chair with his coat. She'd thought her corset would be more of a puzzle, but Simon's hands unlaced her with an air of long practice that she knew ought to have unsettled her. Instead she found herself grateful that someone else had taught him the ways of disrobing a woman, so she did not have to bear his surprise and impatience when confronted with the labyrinthine reality of a lady's undergarments. He rolled her stockings down her legs, lifted her chemise over her head and slid her drawers down to her ankles, and only when she turned to help to undress him did she discover he was already naked.

The shock of that struck her like hot water, just this side of scalding, and she felt the whole of her body tingle with it. She couldn't seem to stop looking at him. He was furred and furrowed and square, as stocky in the waist as in the shoulder. Slowly, he sank to his knees before her.

Anne caught her breath. She never would have thought to ask him to do that. It seemed wrong, perverse in the same way watching him touch himself had felt perverse. And as with that other sight, she felt her body respond, as though a volcano had cracked open inside her, the steam and the heat shimmering through her veins. Firelight flickered over Simon's thick hair and over one shoulder, but her shadow fell across and darkened the rest of him. From that shadow, he reached out one hand and placed it gently on the arch of her foot.

Anne squeaked, an undignified sound of helpless surprise and pleasure. One corner of Simon's mouth lifted in acknowledgement but he didn't look up. His gaze was...somewhat lower. Anne had forgotten her nakedness in appreciation of his, but that was all over now. All at once she became forcefully aware of the softness of her belly, the slight sway of her breasts, the tension in her calves. The building heat in the place between her legs—an arousal she recognized from stolen, lonely nights.

An arousal her husband had promised to satisfy.

He leaned forward and pressed his lips to the soft curve of her hip.

Anne knew she wasn't beautiful. Not to the eyes. For much of her life, she'd thought that was the only kind of beauty. But now, with this man's mouth on her skin, the muscles of his broad back flexing with effort beneath her gaze, she felt a new kind of beauty well up inside her. A beauty that came from within and was not granted by others, a beauty that she could wield rather than something used to define or confine or dismiss her. Beautiful to the touch, and to herself.

Shaking, she threaded her fingers through his hair. The hand he'd rested on her foot moved upward, pausing briefly on her ankle and the tender spot behind her knee. His fingertips slid through the curls between her legs, parting her and causing the breath to catch in the back of her throat. And then his mouth moved, covering her, and his tongue slid over one spot and every muscle in her body seemed to tighten and twist all at once. Anne choked on a groan and clenched her fingers in his hair. Simon took this as encouragement and sped up, sending spikes of pure pleasure from her center, radiating outward along her limbs.

When her knees began to shake she pulled harder on his hair, making him lift his face. "Bed," she insisted.

The sheets were cool against her back, her husband a wall of heat above her. She wrapped her arms around his shoulders as he dipped his head to her breasts and put his mouth to wonderful use on her nipples. Anne writhed in delight and urged him on, whispering encouragement, nonsense, blasphemy—anything to keep him from stopping. It was the most delicious feeling she'd ever known in her life and despite her best intentions her control began to fray. There was a wildness at the edges of her senses, a feeling new and strong and not entirely trustworthy—but before she could find a voice for her worry, she felt Simon's hand move between her legs and he was sliding one finger inside her.

She was wet there, she could tell. Wetter than she had ever been. And hungry, as well, in a way that was as new and frightening as the wildness was. She bore down instinctively on his hand, clenching her inner muscles tight, searching for the satisfaction she knew was there. If she could only find it. "Please," she whispered. "I don't..."

Simon soothed her with a murmur, slipped his hand free and spread her thighs. When he moved his bulk between her legs, Anne raised her head and saw he was hard again, the tip of his— what did he call it?—resting against one of her thighs as he got his weight balanced above her in the bed. She craned her head around to look as he began to push inside her. She'd felt this before but she'd never seen it, and suddenly she wanted—needed —to watch. There was the familiar moment of strain, the stretch she'd come to associate with this part of the act. He blew out a breath and shuddered briefly while Anne tilted her hips slightly to take him further in. He glanced up at her, eyes filled with a mixture of laughter and frustration, and Anne felt a sudden wash of protectiveness that jarred with the restless chitterings of desire. She raised one hand to his cheek. "Don't worry," she said.

Simon laughed out loud at that, the sound tense and thin. "I'm trying not to hurt you."

"Hurt me how?" Even as she asked, he slipped a little deeper inside and there was a new edge to it that had Anne licking her lips. It didn't feel dangerous—or rather, it did, but in a good way. "I think you could be a little braver if you liked," she suggested.

Simon just stared at her for a long moment. The frisson of pleasure began to fade, sparking Anne's irritation at her husband's inexplicable delay. Well, if he wouldn't take charge, she would—she lifted her heels, placed her feet on the back of his thighs, grabbed his shoulders for balance and said, "Now."

Then she pulled at him with her feet.

She didn't move him very far—it was an odd position, one that strained her muscles more than she liked—but the surprise of it was enough. Simon lurched forward, driving into her in one rough plunge. One of the hands that supported him slipped sideways, unbalancing him, and his shoulder came down heavily onto her chest. Anne squeaked at that, but what really drove the breath from her lungs was the sensation of being suddenly, ungently filled. The wildness returned with a vengeance. Her husband had raised his torso again and was trying for some sort of apology. Anne would have none of this. She dug her nails into his shoulders, sucked in the deepest breath she could and said, "Again."

Simon lost all pretense of gentility.

He pulled out and drove back into her, not quickly but with force. She squealed again, tightened her legs around him, and pushed back as hard as she could. Torrents of fire sizzled through her as he continued to thrust, the rasp of his breath becoming grunts and then groans that sounded almost painful. Anne clenched her inner muscles around him and felt him shudder. The back-and-forth of him was tantalizing but it wasn't quite enough. She frowned and tried to urge him faster, but he merely shook his head wordlessly.

Anne cursed at him. Simon cursed back—then one of his hands gripped her hip, thumb digging painfully into the bone. Another moment and he had worked that hand between their bodies, to the spot his mouth had found before. He began stroking her between thrusts, his chest tilted, shoulder hitched up as he brought her roaring back to mindless desperation.

When he began begging her to come for him, with him, just please come, Anne finally arched her back, yelled, and exploded.

The pleasure seemed to shimmer everywhere—inside her, around her, in the ache in her fingers and the breath in her lungs. Simon swore again and dug into her, bucking her up the tousled sheets, pushing as deep as he could while he strained against his own climax. When he jetted inside her, a rush of heat, Anne felt a second crisis take her and bit down on his shoulder hard enough to taste blood.

Afterward she was not surprised to find herself shaking. She usually shook after such pleasures, though they had never been so overwhelming before. She didn't realize, until Simon brushed his thumb against her cheek, that she was crying. That did surprise her. She tried to stop and couldn't quite. The lack of control was frightening. "Don't you dare apologize," she warned her rosy-cheeked husband.

"I won't." He pushed a tangled strand of hair off her forehead. "But if it hurt, you should have told me."

"Didn't this hurt?" she asked, running her finger along the bite mark she'd left on his neck.

His eyes flared with something she couldn't quite name. "Not at the time."

"There you are then." With a grunt he slid free of her body. Anne shook at the sensation—there was a pressure, a little relief and a little pain. She felt sore, though she hadn't felt sore after any of their other nights together. She felt raw and exhausted and exposed, even through the lingering haze of pleasure.

Simon got out of bed and stepped behind a dressing screen, which spared her from having to look him in the face for a few moments. But then he returned with a basin of water, a cloth and the evident intention of cleaning her off. Anne was having none of this—she had gone farther out into the wilderness than she had expected, and every part of her was now crying out for retreat. She reached out and put her hand on his wrist. He stilled at once. "I can do that," she said.

Her nodded and handed her the cloth. She made a few hasty swipes beneath the sheets and returned it to him. He cleaned himself as well, then replaced the basin behind the screen. By the time he stepped back around, Anne had managed to get to her feet, despite the ache of never-used muscles and a persistent sharp twinge in places she had no names for. She had a strong urge to hide, to sort out her thoughts in private before she had to confront his. Something dark and new had happened between them—they had both been a little out of control. It had never happened like that before, and she suspected it wasn't necessarily supposed to happen at all. She had to think.

"Where are you going?" Simon asked.

"My bedroom," she replied, surprised. "Where else?"

He fidgeted, which was a rather more interesting set of gestures on a naked man than on one fully clothed. Anne looked at the twitch in his hands and the tension in his shoulders and felt the now-familiar throb of desire return like a new flame blown from a dying ember. "I thought you might like to stay," Simon said. Her eyes flew up to his face, which was too placid. "Here. With me."

Anne stared at him. "I hadn't thought of that."

"It's already warm here," Simon said. "It could be very pleasant." He swallowed and one of his hands gripped the bedpost hard enough to whiten his knuckles. "If you like."

Good heavens, the man was *nervous*. Anne's soul rose up and rebelled. Her earlier sense of protectiveness returned and redoubled. Whatever had happened between them, it was not something *he* had done to *her*—but if she left, he would believe that and it would slowly poison him. It might even cause him to rethink the whole adventure.

She refused to leave him alone to become prey to self-doubt

and hesitation. Especially not if those fears would prevent them from working out exactly how these new pleasures worked.

It was behavior unbecoming of a countess.

"I should like to stay," Anne said, sinking back down onto the bed. "Thank you for offering."

"You're welcome." Simon started to bow, quite formally, before he caught himself and realized he was still naked. Anne grinned and relaxed back against the pillows as her husband blew out the remaining candles.

She had not shared a bed with another person since she was a very small girl, and her cousin Hecuba had been a very restless sleeper. Simon was not. Simon was huge and heavy, and his weight in the bed made Anne roll into him even if she tried not to. But he gave off nearly as much heat as the fire in the hearth, especially when he pulled the blankets tight around them both. And it was more than pleasant to feel his arm around her waist, tucking her close against him. She would have expected there to be some awkwardness in the proximity—a shoulder-blade in the wrong place, a strange tilt to the neck—but in fact the mutual softness of their flesh seemed to cushion all the bones beneath. Anne rested her hands atop his on her belly and let herself sink into darkness.

CHAPTER 5

*S*imon scooped more eggs onto a plate and leaned back in his chair. Across from him, his wife perched in the sitting room's massive armchair, feet tucked beneath her, wearing a dressing gown in a deep shade of caramel. She was sorting through the enormous pile of invitations a footman had carried in on a silver tray. "There are a great many more than usual," she commented, slicing open one heavy cream-and-gold envelope and pulling out the paper within. Her eyebrows lifted and she choked on her sip of breakfast chocolate. "This one's from the Duchess of Eider!" she sputtered.

"I introduced her last night, if you recall," Simon offered.

His wife fixed him with a stern gaze. "I recall last night in great detail, thank you." Simon was instantly aroused by her sharp and knowing tone, but Anne had already turned her attention back to the swirling scrolls of ink on the page. "I had no idea I had made such an impression on Her Grace." She thumbed through the stack—at least two dozen, by Simon's estimation. "Or any of the others." She pulled out one envelope and brandished it at him. "Mrs. Audley barely tolerated me at the Heathertons' dinner last week. And now she invites me to lunch with her and a select group of intimates?"

"That's quite a victory—she's very well-connected." Simon set his fork and plate on the small table to one side. John the footman at once began to gather breakfast's remains, though Anne kept hold of her cup of chocolate. Simon wondered what she tasted like with chocolate on her tongue, and made sure to formally dismiss the footman. "In fact," he continued when they were alone, "it's precisely what you hoped to gain by marrying me."

Anne scowled and set her cup on the table with a sharp rap. "Let me remind you, sir, that marriage was your idea, not mine."

Simon blinked at the sudden storm. "Of course it was."

"Then you needn't make me sound so mercenary," she went on.

"Not mercenary," he protested. "Practical. Reasoned. Thoughtful." Anne relaxed again, though she retained an aggravated crease between her brows. Would it smooth out and become placid again if he kissed her there? He wasn't quite brash enough to try. "And now you've achieved your practical, reasoned, thoughtful goal, for the good of yourself and your family."

She looked at him, her brown eyes dark with unease. "But I've done nothing, really," she protested.

Of course, Simon thought, realizing why she was puzzled. He had been so struck by her fundamental capability that he'd forgotten Anne was not used to the ways of society among the very wealthy and highly titled. It was a rarefied, only intermittently pleasant world with its own peculiar rules, similar but not identical to the respectable gentility in which his countess had been brought up. "That was precisely why you succeeded," he explained. "You did nothing. That is what has won them over."

The crease between her brows returned with a vengeance. "Do you always make so little sense so early in the day?"

Simon chuckled and leaned forward, elbows on his knees. "When you were at the Heathertons' dinner, you went out of your way to be pleasing, didn't you?"

"You know I did," she returned. "You were there."

He nodded. "So I was. And you did your very best to make friends with every other guest."

Her scowl deepened. "What was I supposed to do—deliberately offend?"

"Do you think you offended anyone at the Morleys' last night?" he pushed.

She started to speak, then paused. He could practically see the thoughts racing through her mind. "No," she said. "I was, however, very distracted." She turned those thoughtful eyes on him. "By you."

"By me," Simon agreed. Her gaze had set his blood to simmering again, but that could wait. Last night must seem...strange to her, and he refused to let haste or impatience push him into discomfiting her further. "So instead of trying to please everyone, you stayed pleasantly distant. Cordially aloof."

"I didn't feel aloof at all," his wife returned, but she was starting to smile at him, just a little.

"You didn't act as though you needed them."

Anne laughed. "I was too busy needing you."

There was true warmth in her voice now, and the last of Simon's tension dissolved at the sound. He rose from his chair, stepped across the small expanse of carpet and knelt in front of her. She sat straight up in the armchair, eyes glowing just as they had when he'd done this last night, *sans* clothes. He didn't know quite why it pleased her, but he was willing to be mystified if it meant she would flush and lick her lips at him as she was doing right now. "I needed you too," he said, then lifted her hand and kissed the back of it like a troubadour paying homage to his lady muse. He felt her other hand come to rest on his cheek and looked up to find her smiling indulgently at him. The tender gesture, the light in her eyes, the curve of her lips completely undid him. Wordless, he pressed another kiss to her palm, giddy and grateful beyond all reason.

She caught her breath at the touch of his mouth and he felt her pulse jump in the veins beneath her skin. And then she was bending forward and leaning down and sliding off the stiff leather of the chair, and then his arms were full of caramel wool and his mouth had been claimed by hers. She straddled him there on the carpet, her thighs sliding perfectly over his hips, and despite the fact that he'd come twice last night he knew all she had to do was lift up all that wool and slide onto him and he would come again at her command. Her mouth was rich with the taste of chocolate, but more intoxicating was her own scent, ripening in her hair and on her unbathed skin. He'd dreamed of her all night, his face resting against her neck as they slept, his hands filled with the soft flesh of her belly and breasts.

She pushed against his chest and Simon obediently fell back. When he tried to pull her after him, she shook her head and put a hand on his chest. "Don't move," she said.

Simon went still. Of course he could move if he wanted to. He outweighed her by several stone at least, and despite her superior position atop him he knew he could sweep her beneath him and plunge inside her as easily as breathing. She would probably enjoy it—he had finesse enough to see to that.

But it wasn't what she'd asked of him. And there was something so pure and perfect and pleasing in doing what she asked, despite all his own desires and inclinations, that he wanted to bask in it like a lizard in the sun. So he put his hands down flat on the carpet and tried to control the heaving of his chest while his wife worked open the belt on his dressing gown. The heavy red brocade fell away from his hips easily enough, but she had to push it aside to bare his chest. He hadn't worn anything beneath it, since he'd planned on dressing immediately after breakfast, and now he was absurdly grateful for that lazy impulse. Because here he lay now, panting, his cock hard beneath her weight, his heart hammering so fast he worried it would burst from his chest and kill him.

Not even that sudden, irrational fear was enough to make him move. Not with his wife, wrapped in that sweet caramel color, taking such obvious pleasure in having him laid out like a banquet beneath her.

Anne trailed her fingers through the hair on his chest and hummed. "I love looking at you," she said. "Looking is safe. I don't lose track of myself when I'm just looking. Touching, too, is lovely—at first." She skimmed her hand lower, to his waist. Simon's belly tightened beneath her touch and his hands flexed at his sides, but otherwise he managed to keep himself still for her. "What we did last night...it shocked me a little. Frightened me. I had felt pleasure before but I had always felt in control of it. In control of me. Last night the pleasure overwhelmed me. It was memorable but it was not entirely comfortable."

"I am sorry," Simon said. His neck was starting to ache a little from the angle he had to hold it at to look at her properly. He'd be damned before he'd let that shift him.

Anne smiled and bent to take his nipple into her mouth. He gasped as her tongue circled him lazily before she straightened again. Putting herself at a distance. "It was not your fault," she said. "It was mine. I let things get out of hand when I should have been in control of myself."

Simon shook his head. "I took control from you without asking. I thought about pleasing your body and I forgot to please your mind." *Or your heart*, he thought to say, but didn't. "I could make up for that."

Anne went still, her eyes intent on his. "How do you mean?"

"You need to be in control," Simon said. "So you shall be in control." She still just looked at him, wary. "So for instance, when you tell me not to move," he flicked his gaze to his hands and back at her, "I won't move."

"As simple as that?"

"As simple as that."

She cocked her head, considering. "You would let me lead, even though you are the more experienced in these matters?"

Simon grimaced. "My experience is not extensive. I have not been particularly profligate," he said. "My younger brother used to despair at my general indifference to debauchery—and I always thought he was debauched enough for us both. Besides, as I told you, the only experiences that matter now are the ones you and I share." Because he was human and his ego was stinging a little, he ventured to ask, "Was there anything from last night that you *did* particularly enjoy?"

"I liked it when you used your mouth on me," she said.

Her gaze was so nakedly hungry that he had to grit his teeth against the bolt of lust that struck him. "I could do that again," he said when he could speak. "Right now. If it would please you."

Anne's hand tensed on his skin, the points of her nails briefly starring his skin. "I would like that very much," she said. Her tone was cool and formal but Simon wasn't fooled. She was defending herself—against him, against her own desire, it didn't matter. She was in command and she wanted his mouth.

He put his hands on the hem of her dressing gown. "May I?" She nodded, and he slipped his hands beneath the fabric to the soft skin of her thighs. Soothing circles, gentle passes with his thumb, until he felt her muscles start to relax beneath the attention. She tensed again when his hands climbed higher, and he paused. "Would you prefer to be in the chair or shall I stay like this?"

She thought for a moment. "In the chair," she said, "but I am going to lock the door." She rose to her feet and did as she'd said. Simon pushed himself to his knees and stayed there, determined to be patient. His instincts and the long habit of responsibility were urging him to take over, to take charge, but more than anything he wanted her to feel safe, and that was not the way to do it. He could stand a little discomfort of his own, to ease hers.

She wasn't entirely at ease yet, that much was obvious. She took her seat in the chair stiffly, as though at a tribunal. Toes clenched, ankles together, hands fisted on knees. "You may begin," she said.

He wanted to laugh. He wanted to kiss her. But Simon did

neither. He merely leaned forward and pressed his cheek against the side of her calf.

It was an instinctual move, a gesture of pure submission and trust. But it worked— even through the thickness of her dressing gown he could feel the tension ebb out of her. He circled her ankle with one hand, his breath gusting warmly around his fingers, and slowly—almost casually—he began to lift the hem of her skirt.

By the time he bared her knees, Anne was flushed and breathing quickly. Simon pressed a kiss to the soft skin on the side of her right knee, then looked up. "May I continue?"

For a moment she simply looked at him, her breath coming fast, her chest heaving up and down. Then she visibly gathered herself, lifted her chin and spread her legs wider for him. "Please do."

Simon thrilled at the combination of her vulnerability and power, but reminded himself that he was going to go slowly and not let himself get carried away as he had before. He took a deep breath and slid the fabric of her dressing gown higher, all the way to her hips. She was beautiful in the morning light, rosy as the dawn—but he felt her muscles go tense again beneath his hands.

She was nervous about him looking at her.

Well that was fine. She'd been clear about what she wanted. Someday he would make sure to tell her how beautiful her cunt was, but for now Simon had a different goal in mind.

He bent his head to taste her.

She tasted as rich as he remembered from last night, the scent of her rising around him as he slid tender fingers through the dark curls that cloaked her. She gasped when his mouth touched her and shook when his tongue began to move. He worked her rhythmically, reverently, every sense attuned to the tiny movements and breathless moans he wrung from her. His hands slipped beneath her ass, holding her tight as her cunt grew impossibly wet—her own liquid or his, it didn't matter. He redoubled his efforts and her fingers tangled in his hair. Before long she was pushing her hips forward against him, sliding down to a slouch in the armchair and throwing her legs over his shoulders.

"Harder," she demanded.

Simon obeyed. He slipped a single finger inside her channel and began to curl it, pressing up against the rippling muscles while his tongue circled back to her clitoris and strummed against it as hard as he could.

Anne bowed up against him and came, gushing over him. Simon reveled in it, in the heat and the shaking and the soft cries she made, the tightness of her thighs against his shoulders and the clutch of her fingers in his hair. It was as though a bell sounded somewhere in the depths of his soul—the purest, clearest note he'd ever heard, reverberating through him and setting him trembling.

With a sigh, Anne relaxed. She pushed herself up and untangled her limbs from his. Her face was bright red, her hair a tangle, her eyes wide and bright. Simon could remember thinking she was plain, in the same way he could remember the ache of the fever he'd survived when he was seven. Both memories felt as though they'd happened to different people altogether.

His wife leaned down and kissed him. She tasted different after her climax, somehow earthier, and he wasn't ready for the kiss to end when she pulled away. "That was marvelous," she said. "Thank you."

"Did you feel more like yourself that time?" Simon asked.

She nodded, and traced her finger along the line of his jaw. Her brow lowered. "But what about you?"

Simon shrugged this aside. "You can deal with me later. Tonight if you like. Or this afternoon if you're feeling impatient." Anne laughed and Simon grinned back at her. He was still rock hard, but that didn't matter. She wanted children, and he was the only way she was going to get them. His turn would come. This morning was hers.

He was hers.

The thought settled onto him, light but shocking, like a

snowflake on bare skin. It felt like the first flake in a coming avalanche, ominous and life-altering, so Simon was more than a little relieved when Anne stood up, tied her dressing gown properly about her waist and began sorting through her pile of invitations. Simon followed suit, though his unspent cock tented out his robe in a comical manner. "I'll have to answer some of these at once," his wife said, then pulled out one plain envelope, much less ornate than the others. "This one is addressed to you," she said easily and handed it over.

Simon recognized the angles and flourishes of his former mistress's handwriting.

The world seemed to freeze around him.

Anne was oblivious to his shock. She picked up the tray of invitations, gave him another sloe-eyed smile—which Simon did his best to return—and departed for her bedroom. No doubt her maid was already there, waiting to help the countess bathe and garb herself in one of the many gowns that seemed perfectly designed to bedevil her hapless husband.

Simon was left alone Fiona's letter.

If he knew one thing with any certainty, it was this—nothing good would come of opening that letter. How could it?

After a long moment, he tossed it unread into the fire.

CHAPTER 6

The next two months were the busiest of Anne's life.

She was received by the Duchess of Eider, and tutored in carnal vocabulary by her ardent husband. She knew many more names for their various parts now, and was engaged in practicing which ones she liked best and which ones made Simon gasp and growl and go hard when she whispered them at inappropriate moments. She attended a country house picnic given by Mrs. Audley, and was delightfully ravished against a tree when Simon returned from the hunt with the other husbands. She visited the earl in his study, fucked him until his eyes crossed, and was presentable again in time to have dinner with Lady Morley, Mrs. Bell, and a Russian princess who was Mrs. Bell's third cousin by marriage. And these events were merely the brightest stars in a constellation of other gatherings—dinners and parties and teas and balls given by lesser lights, for larger crowds, who knew the end of the Season was approaching and with it London's long period of social stagnation. Anne was able to introduce her mother and father and sister to enough of her new acquaintance that the family's blackened reputation began to flake away like a coat of old paint. The new countess knew a moment of unalloyed triumph when Evangeline, haloed in smiles, informed her that Mr. Bertram Egley had made her an offer and been accepted.

Simon offered his congratulations and Mrs. Pym dissolved in happy tears.

Anne hugged first her glowing sister, then the beaming Mr. Egley. "I'm so happy for you both," she said. "Have you fixed a date for the wedding yet?"

Evangeline tucked her arm into the crook of her fiancé's elbow. "Actually," she said, "that depends on you and Simon." Mr. Egley looked suddenly nervous, and Evangeline patted his hand soothingly, then turned back to her sister. "Would you mind very much if we were married from Rushmore House?"

"It sets a more elegant tone," Mrs. Pym hastened to add.

Anne looked to Simon. He smiled and touched her shoulder briefly. "It's up to you, my dear," he said.

In all her recent busyness, Anne had yet to host any events of her own. She'd almost forgotten it was even possible—that she was allowed to invite other ladies to join her for food and conversation—but she had to admit the idea had appeal. She took her sister's hands and kissed her cheek. "I would be honored."

It was only on the way home, when her husband was just starting to kiss the most sensitive part of her neck, that another thought occurred to her. "Simon?" she asked, with what breath she still had, "why is it that you've never had your friends over for dinner since we've been married?"

"And have them all clamoring to seduce you away from me?" She snorted and he chuckled. "It's quite simple," he said, pausing to lick his hot tongue briefly against her delicate earlobe. "I haven't any friends."

Anne went cold and pulled away, staring. Simon seemed serious, calm, as though he'd made a trivial remark on the late arrival of crocuses this spring. He tried to bend down to kiss her again but her hand on his chest stopped him. "No friends at all?" she asked.

He shrugged. "I have a rather large acquaintance. There are

men I know from my school years, their wives and families. There are the men at my club. There is the artistic set my brother used to run with—"

"Who are not precisely respectable."

"And who therefore we could not associate with."

"Of course we could," Anne countered. "Just not on the same night as Lady Morley or Mrs. Bell." She toyed with the end of her husband's cravat.

He caught her hand in his. "And Lady Morley and Mrs. Bell—would you consider them your friends already? After a few short weeks?"

"Lady Morley has a sweet temper and a good heart," Anne returned. "And Mrs. Bell is one of the wittiest conversationalists I've ever met—she must know a thousand ways of drawing someone out and putting them at their ease. They aren't good friends yet, but they might be, given time. For the present I have Evangeline and Hecuba, and a handful of cousins and a few girls from the neighborhood where we grew up, whom I still write to fairly frequently. And my mother, I suppose," she added.

"Does family count then?" Simon leaned back, one long arm stretched out along the top of the seat. "I suppose I have had friends, then. I had John up until recently, so the house never felt empty. I wrote to Imogen occasionally in the course of her travels with my aunt. I've been meaning to write to her again, but you and I have been a little...preoccupied lately." His tone was more than suggestive, in tandem with the mischievous tilt to his mouth.

Anne gave him her most quelling glance. She would not be distracted until she was good and ready.

Simon looked away, gaslight from outside the coach spreading dappled light over his face. "It's very strange, inheriting a title. You grow up knowing you were born for a purpose, that all your education and instruction is designed to make you fit your proper place, like a gear in a clock that must be cut and polished just so if the whole machine is to keep accurate time. John had it easier—all his mischief and mistakes could be shrugged aside with a laugh and a roguish wink. 'You know how younger sons are,' they said. But every prank I pulled, every small act of rebellion or disobedience was a noticeable blot on the family name, a reminder that I was letting down not only my own father but his dead father and all the other dead fathers and brothers who'd come before. I would imagine the whole parade, shaking their ghostly heads and roving up and down the ancestral hallways, moaning in disappointment." He laughed, but Anne did not join him. "So I avoided trouble, or anyone who looked like trouble, or anyone who had even a nodding acquaintance with trouble. Which was pretty much everyone."

"Except for your brother," Anne said softly.

The earl's lip's quirked. "And I managed to foul that up rather spectacularly too." The pain in his eyes flared briefly and then was hidden away.

So he was unhappy with the estrangement, even though he felt he had to preserve it. No wonder he'd responded when she expressed a desire to fix the whole mess. Anne might as well have offered water to a man dying of thirst. Simon had done precisely as he'd promised—Anne had been accepted by Society, Evangeline's future was assured and Mr. and Mrs. Pym would soon be welcoming wedding guests to one of the most fashionable homes in London.

He'd given her everything—even some things she hadn't known she wanted. Trust and passion and patience. Maybe even something approaching love.

All at once, Anne was determined to give him everything in return. The friends he'd denied himself for so long. The family he'd come to see as a judge and jury, rather than as a source of affection and support. The child he needed, not simply as an heir but as someone he could protect and lavish attention on. Their marriage might be barely a month old, but it was clear to Anne that her husband had a deep and abiding need to cherish those he cared about. The way he'd tried to atone for his mistakes and his brother's. The way he'd learned to take care of her. To make her feel as though she could be herself both in bed and out. Anne had been trying so hard to play the role of the perfect wife, then the perfect lover—both roles submissive and demure and yielding, none of which traits were particularly prominent in her character. She was stubborn and demanding and stern, and somehow Simon had found a way to put those charmless traits to good carnal use.

She would employ them now for his sake as well as her own.

Simon must have caught the steely glint in her eye, because he spoke again. "Please, Anne," he said. "Do not make me a project. I will try to broaden my own acquaintance in my own time. Promise me."

Her meddlesome nature rebelled at this, but her rational side acknowledged the request was fair. "I promise," she said, leaned forward and kissed her husband. Distraction proceeded apace.

Unfortunately, despite Anne's wickedest intentions, their return home coincided with the disappointing discovery that her courses had begun. She'd been so hoping to conceive quickly— they had certainly been trying with enough frequency—but the telltale minor cramping, backache and shameful stains on her pantaloons were arguments she couldn't counter. By tomorrow afternoon she knew she'd be racked with pain, doubled up beneath the blankets in her bed, an extra hot brick tucked against her aching back. Her mother, sister and cousin had never suffered so much during their monthlies—though her mother had often fallen victim to blistering headaches that sometimes lasted for days. A woman's curse, she'd called it. "I'll have Grace draw me a bath in my room," she sighed, cheeks flushing as she informed her husband.

"You could," Simon said genially. "Or you could have your bath here, where there's already a fire." He began kneading her shoulders, dropping gentle kisses on the back of her neck.

Anne leaned back into the caress. Despite the ache in her lower belly, she was still full of a sharp hunger she'd quite looked forward to satisfying. "Are you sure?" she asked.

"I am," Simon murmured, and rang for the bath.

Less than an hour later, Anne was sinking into a steaming tub with a sigh of relief. The hot water set her tingling, but not as much as the feel of her husband's hands sliding over her skin as she leaned back against the side of the bathtub. Simon had stripped down to his shirtsleeves and taken up a kneeling position at her back, a wall of warmth and solidity pressing against the top of her shoulders. Anne sleepily admired the strength of his bared wrist and forearm while his hand moved lower and lower on her body. He played and pinched at her nipples, while his mouth and tongue made lazy patterns on her neck, banishing tension and making her breath catch in her throat. He seemed as patient as a mountain, waiting out the eons while his hands woke and eased and soothed her tense muscles. Her cunt too was rather tender, so that she winced a little when he slid one finger inside her, but Simon stayed slow, teasing her clitoris with gentle circles, his other hand clasped tight around her shoulder. By this time he knew well enough how to best make her come, so Anne simply relaxed and let herself drift on the soft sounds of moving water and the in-and-out sounds of two people breathing. It was an impossibly safe feeling, being so held and encircled, and she closed her eyes and sighed and at length tumbled into a sweet and easy climax that seemed never to end.

"Better?" Simon asked. She could feel the smile on his mouth as he pressed his lips against her shoulder.

"Much," Anne said. Simon began stripping out of his trousers and shirt, which was now soaked to the shoulder. Anne looked at him through the haze of satisfied pleasure and rose to her knees in the tub. "I think there's room, if you'd care to join me," she said.

Simon raised an eyebrow, considering size and volume. One corner of his mouth quirked up.

It was awkward at first, all knees and elbows and moments when gravity seemed to turn itself briefly sideways. Both Anne and Simon lost balance more than once, and Anne got a mouthful of bathwater when she laughed at the startled look on her husband's face as his left knee went out from under him. But by the time she was done sputtering he'd positioned himself below her, put his hands on her waist, and was sliding her cunt down the ready length of his cock.

Anne threw her head back. "Yes, that's it," she moaned.

Simon laughed softly against the heated skin of her neck. Anne tried to raise herself, to feel that hard shaft thrusting inside her, but he held her in place, one hand slipping down to stroke her clitoris. She shuddered, still caught up in the aftershocks, and Simon's sturdy body shook beneath her. His hold eased slightly, just enough to allow her motion but not so much that it gave her back full control. She could have commanded him to release her, to let her set the pace, but the tension between her galloping desire and the slow, deliberate pace he held her to was more intoxicating than she could have predicted. The pads of his fingers sank into the soft flesh of her hip, hard enough to ache but not hard enough to bruise. Time dilated and spun into epochs as she fucked him, his mouth on her breasts, his fingers between her legs, her nails scoring his shoulders and the back of his neck. A low, rolling climax eventually shook a gasp out of her, clenching her inner muscles and twisting her gut with pleasure deep and dark. Simon's control slipped its leash for just one moment—he bucked up hard against her and came, gripping her with both hands, his breath rough against her collarbone. She buried her face in his hair and inhaled as steam rose around them.

Anne smiled and skimmed her lips across his ear. "Thank you," she murmured.

"It was my pleasure." Simon wheezed a laugh as his climax eased off. They separated and toweled each other dry—for the most part—then rang for the servants to remove the tub and the bathwater.

Thus soothed and ready for bed, Anne found a comfortable rest for her head on Simon's shoulder. Soon the soft buzz of his sleeping breath could be heard rumbling through his body beside hers. Anne stayed awake for a few more minutes, thinking. She'd long since given up being shocked by anything she and Simon did with or to one another, but that did not mean she couldn't still be surprised. She always felt pricklier than usual during her courses —even aside from the physical discomfort, the general sense of...uncleanliness...that accompanied these six to eight days always slipped beneath her skin and made her unusually cross. But Simon had touched her as he always did, with that combination of demand and reverence that never failed to move her profoundly. It was a gift unlooked-for, and all the more precious because of it.

She was determined surprise him in return.

She was determined to give him a family.

Visions of cherubic offspring and the pattering of tiny feet filled her dreams.

CHAPTER 7

"*E*vangeline rather likes the rose color, but as for myself I think the pale blue would stand out so much better against the decorations in the morning room..." Mrs. Pym had spread every last one of her fashion plates across every couch in Anne's front parlor. A great debate was being undertaken as to the merits of each individual style, cut, color, fabric, and trim. And since Anne had long exhausted all her opinions on the subject, Mrs. Pym was now forced to carry both sides of the argument forward, with great effort and concentration.

Anne sipped her tea and hoped it could scald all the sharp responses from her tongue. She had planned a leisurely afternoon to meet with the cook and the butler regarding menus and wine selections for the coming week, including a small tea for a few select friends. She thought it wise to try hosting a small event before attempting a larger one, even one purely for family. Evangeline's wedding breakfast was going to be a challenge, and Anne wanted more preparation than she'd had. What's more, she had numerous notes and letters to write and invitations to answer —a countess's correspondence was never-ending, she had learned. But then Mrs. Pym had showed up, pale of face and tremulous of voice, citing an urgent complaint about the wedding arrangements—which puzzled her daughter, since no arrangements presently existed to her knowledge. Anne had infelicitously not foreseen that this excuse was but a pretext to gain entrance, and now her mother had seized the front parlor as her own and made it the command headquarters of her own very personal, fashionable war.

"Do you have enough champagne laid by, dear?" Mrs. Pym was now asking.

"I should think so," said Anne.

Her mother's lips pursed. "We should make very certain—nothing is so tepid as a wedding without champagne!" Despite Anne's forthright objections, Mrs. Pym then insisted upon ringing for the maid and sending her for the butler and sending the butler to the cellar to make an exact count of the number of bottles, their vintage and the order in which they should be served.

Anne thought about screaming with frustration. It was all too easy to imagine her mother responding to such an outburst with a shake of her head and an admonition that she was a lady, not a hoyden. Which would only make Anne scream the harder. And then her head would explode. And some poor scullery maid would have to clean the mess from the ancestral Underwood carpet. And when Simon asked how his wife had died, Mrs. Pym would shake her head again and say that Anne had brought it on herself.

Mrs. Pym had moved on to a fluttery yellow gown with a thousand and one ruffles—Anne thought sourly that it would make Evangeline look like a lemon trifle, which admittedly Bertram Egley might enjoy—when John the footman came in, having taken Phillips' place at the front door. "If you please, my lady," he said, "there's a woman just arrived who insists on being seen." The stiffness of his expression caught Anne's attention: he looked as though he'd accidentally swallowed a lemon but was determined to pretend that no such fruit existed.

Before her daughter could ask for further information, her mother interrupted. "Oh!" cried Mrs. Pym. "Of course she may come in." She waved John away, then began fussing over the wrinkles in her skirt. "You didn't tell me you were expecting company, Anne! Is it Lady Morley? Mrs. Bell?"

"Neither," Anne said. She rubbed a little at her forehead but she knew that mere touch was not going to banish the tension there. Not when the source sat across from her, humming happily and clearing a space for the new arrival.

"Mrs. Fiona Walker." The young lady John ushered in was blonde and beautiful in a quiet, English rose kind of way. She looked to be around five-and-twenty years old. Her gown was dark green and high quality, but not in the first tier of fashion, and though her lips were lovely they were pressed into a thin, anxious line. She paused on the threshold, eyes darting between Anne and Mrs. Pym, and in her arms...

In her arms, wrapped in a thick woolen blanket, was a child. A child who looked exactly like Simon.

Anne felt as though she were breathing in ice instead of air. The sharp cold cut her to the heart.

"Do sit down, my dear!" Mrs. Pym crowed, patting the newly opened spot on the sofa beside her. Anne remained frozen, and after another wary glance Mrs. Walker moved carefully across the room, fashion plates drifting like leaves in the wake of her belled skirts. She didn't so much sit as perch on the edge of the sofa, a nervous attitude that showed she knew quite well she had entered a world in which she did not belong. Mrs. Pym began a determined fusillade of small talk, to which Mrs. Walker silently submitted.

Anne couldn't tear her eyes away from the child. The resemblance to Simon was truly uncanny. The square cast to the jaw, the broad forehead, the dark hair and eyes... If the babe had had a mustache, Anne would have thought some witch had shrunk her husband down to miniature, the better to carry him around where she wished.

Phillips reappeared at this point to supply Mrs. Pym with the total number of bottles of champagne, which was clearly many more than could be drunk in any one morning by any number of guests. "That will have to do," granted Mrs. Pym, in tones of high skepticism. "Now regarding claret..."

As the butler effectively absorbed Mrs. Pym's attention, Mrs. Walker turned to Anne with real regret in her large blue eyes. "I'm so sorry, my lady," she murmured. Her voice was dulcet, as low and sweet as a lyre. "I never meant to trouble you. I tried to write to Simon—to his lordship—but he never—"

Anne cut her off with the abrupt gesture of one hand. Her stomach churned like a kicked hive full of angry bees, and a thousand hasty words clustered on her tongue. They were not at all the sort of words one spoke in front of innocent children or respectable if overbearing mothers. The child squelched up his— or her?—face and made a small sound, a test cry to see if the world was listening. Its mother bounced it a little and made shushing noises.

Anne wondered if it were possible to snap one's own neck from rage and humiliation.

The baby quieted again, eyes drifting closed with one last little sigh. Anne was seeing spots in the corner of her vision and forced herself to take a deep breath. Then another. A third breath gave her enough air to finally speak. "Phillips," she said, ruthlessly interrupting her mother mid-thought, "perhaps you would be so good as to show Mrs. Pym to the cellar so she may make a thorough inventory of all the wines she might like to serve as part of the menu?"

Phillips' cheeks went pale even as Mrs. Pym clapped her hands with delight. "That is much more efficient!" she said. Phillips bowed in obedience and led her away. Perhaps it was unethical to inflict her mother upon the servants, but Anne's reserves of forbearance had been stretched to their breaking point. There was a larger crisis to deal with now.

The butler preceded a still-chattering Mrs. Pym out of the door. Silence piled up, as stiff and fragile as meringue. The baby turned a little but remained sleeping. Anne's heart thundered in her breast.

"We've known each other for two years, the earl and I." That dulcet voice again. It was an effort for Anne to wrench her eyes up to meet the other woman's. Mrs. Walker's expression was solemn, guarded. "He told me he was getting married and we...made arrangements."

Anne had to try three times before her voice would work. "For the child?"

"No." The blonde woman's hand stroked her child's hair absently, a gesture of long practice. Anne clenched her own hands into fists. "He didn't know about the child. I didn't know myself, not until after the earl had already broken with me. I wrote three times, to tell him, to ask him...to ask him what he thought, really. It seemed cruel not to let him know he had a son."

A son. A boy who would have been an heir, a viscount, had he not been born on the wrong side of the blanket. Any subsequent children Anne had would steal this child's birthright from him by law, if not by chronology. Ancient estates had been destroyed by children like this, Anne knew. Crowns had been stolen and fields washed with blood, castles laid waste and villages burned.

The dark-haired boy, still sleeping, shoved his fist into his mouth.

It was so absurd that Anne could have shouted. She could feel the outrage rising again, choking her—but she throttled it back down. After all, Mrs. Walker was a mother, concerned for the welfare of her child. She was behaving herself quite well, considering the circumstances. How much of a threat could she be? Simon had never even thought to mention her. "What is it you propose?" Anne asked.

Mrs. Walker lifted her head. Those blue eyes had some steel in them, Anne did not fail to note. "I would like to hear whether the earl wishes to acknowledge his son. Not publicly but just to the boy himself," she hastened to add, before Anne could conquer her shock. "I would like to know if he wishes to make some provision for the child's future, or if he prefers that I raise the boy with no knowledge about his paternity. It is entirely up to him."

Anne's stomach twisted at the thought. Family was everything, especially to a child. "Do you have," she groped for a genteel euphemism, "a stable means of support?"

"The earl has signed a contract granting me an annuity," the woman murmured, blushing a little.

Anne had scant time to wonder that a woman of her profession could still blush at anything before the door swung open. Mrs. Pym had returned. "Now if we could only solve this problem with the gown, we could move on to the food—"

"Mother," Anne said. Helplessness and frustration clouded her vision, a storm gathering lightning and looking for somewhere to hurl its bolts.

"—would really need more than six courses—"

"Mother!" Anne tried again. The storm billowed higher.

"Perhaps something a bit more robust than fish?—"

Anne's head snapped up and her eyes narrowed. Patience, never her most abundant resource, finally burned away. Now there was only an evil, gleeful energy, an anticipation of the wounds she knew she was going to inflict as soon as she opened her mouth. Her lips parted as a hot breath filled her.

But before she could speak, Mrs. Walker stood up from the couch. The woman's blue eyes had gone steely again, though her expression remained tranquil. "Would you hold him, my lady?" said the woman, and deposited the baby in Anne's hastily lifted arms. Anne could only gape as the woman—her husband's *former mistress*—a *courtesan*—ably and tactfully steered Anne's mother out of the door, murmured something to John the footman and returned to the sofa. "I told the footman to lock your mother out until you say otherwise," she explained. The barest hint of a smile curled the corners of her rosy lips. She folded her hands and waited for Anne's reaction, as demure as a princess in a painting.

Anne was seized by a wild urge to laugh. Maybe Hecuba and John's misadventure had inured her to scandal. Because surely there was nothing more shocking than for a courtesan to evict a respectable society matron and have the footman bar the door to her. But the only emotion Anne currently recognized of the hundreds spinning about inside her was relief, pure and torrential. For the first time since her mother's arrival this afternoon, Anne felt as though she had room to think properly.

In her arms, the boy opened his eyes and gurgled.

Anne caught her breath. His hair was barely more than a wisp, yet so dark. His eyes roved around, fixed on nothing—but he was young yet. Focus would come, she knew that much. She touched a fingertip to his hand as it opened and closed. How on earth could fingernails be so small yet so recognizable as fingernails? It didn't seem possible. He smelled of laundry and milk and something strangely vegetable, which was at odds with the meaty rolls of fat on his arms and his dumpling cheeks. The boy reached up with one hand and clamped his tiny fingers around hers. Anne fought back a sudden sob, as though he'd grabbed her heart instead of her hand.

What wouldn't she do for him, if he were hers? Mrs. Walker may have barged into the house today, but Anne had done precisely that herself not long ago. She would be a hypocrite to criticize. And she hadn't had the moral force of maternal protectiveness urging her on. How much more aggressive would she have been if she'd been doing it for so small and fragile a creature?

"He's very sweet, isn't he?" The blonde woman may have retaken her seat on the sofa but she still perched only on the edge. Still anxious, because her newborn son was in the arms of her former lover's titled, wealthy, socially powerful wife.

"He is," Anne agreed. The boy released her finger and she smoothed his hair. It was softer than down, strands of gossamer beneath her fingertips. "Does he have a name?"

"Nicholas."

"It suits him." Anne gained control of herself and returned the child to his mother, trying to ignore the hollow inward pang as the boy's weight vanished from her arms. The baby fussed slightly until his mother cooed at him, her face briefly glowing with irrepressible love.

It was the motherly look that cut Anne's heart. That and the gratitude still swimming about in her veins. "We seem to have botched the introductions," she said, extending a hand. "Anne Rushmore, Countess of Underwood."

The woman took her offered hand with only a slight hesitation. "An honor, my lady ."

Anne groped for the etiquette but there really was none to cover the situation. A frank query was required. "Will you stay until Simon returns? He shouldn't be much longer."

The blonde woman hazarded a smile. "I promise to be a more patient guest than your mother," she said.

Anne snorted. "That is a very low bar indeed. What good is being a countess if you have to suffer the same irritations you did when you were a mere miss?" Anne rose to her feet. "My mother has occupied enough of my time this afternoon. Allow me just a few moments to make my farewells and then we can talk more about what is to be done." She paused in the doorway. "Would you like something to eat? Tea? Something for the boy?"

"No, thank you," Mrs. Walker said.

Anne nodded, girt her loins and left the room.

She evicted her mother by the simple expedient of repeating herself. "I'm sorry, but it's time for you to go." She listened to no pleas and she brooked no contradictions.

Phillips helped, with a shade of eagerness Anne had never seen in him. When the door finally closed and Mrs. Pym's hackney rolled away down the drive, Anne and the butler gave simultaneous sighs of relief.

She grinned at him and he went full red. "My apologies, my lady," he said.

"No need, Phillips," Anne returned. "I promise not to inflict her upon you like that again if I can help it."

The butler bowed his thanks. "A few more notes have arrived

in the past hour, my lady," he said, and showed her the silver tray with its creamy parchment offerings.

Anne heaved a sigh. "I'll have to attend to those later, Phillips —we still have one visitor, after all."

The earl arrived home an hour later. Anne was holding Nicholas again—the boy had napped and nursed and was now making sounds he obviously thought were words. To the end of her days, Anne would never forget the look of pure bewilderment on her husband's face when he walked into the parlor and saw his wife holding a baby and chatting with his former mistress.

Anne stood up before he had recovered enough to speak. Mrs. Walker stood with her, all her good humor fading into apprehension. Anne handed Nicholas to his mother and patted her reassuringly on the shoulder. "Go ahead," she urged gently. "Tell him."

The woman didn't hesitate, which further raised her in Anne's estimation. "I would like to introduce you to your son, my lord," said Mrs. Walker.

Simon goggled at the boy, who goggled right back. Anne would have laughed if it hadn't been for the ache in her chest. She watched the earl stretch out his hands, watched Mrs. Walker hold out her son, watched the baby settle comfortably in the crook of his father's arm and blow bubbles of spit from his tiny baby lips. Reverently, Simon put out a finger and touched his son's cheek, the gesture an echo of Anne's. The boy waved his arms and arched his back with grumpy sounds.

Simon's breathing stopped. Just for a moment but it was enough. Anne recognized the look on his face as he stared down at his son—love and no mistake. Shaded by wonder and surprise, perhaps, but as clear as the dawn.

Anne Rushmore, née Pym, had always wanted a family. Marrying Simon had intensified that yearning, especially once she'd noticed how lonely her husband was and how much he would benefit from a pack of lively, intelligent children. She had some experience with envy before this—when other daughters of the *ton* had better gowns or better figures or better fortunes, when her cousin's fire and her sister's sweetness had been more admired than Anne's prickly frankness, when Hecuba and John had finally sorted themselves out and embarked on what appeared to be a lifetime of unadulterated bliss. But those had been pinpricks in comparison to this fatal stab through the heart—Anne had never felt as viscerally, nakedly covetous as she felt right then, while her husband cradled his firstborn son and the mother hovered nearby trying not to appear anxious.

Such envy would gain her nothing. She could have hysterics quite easily if she wanted—the roil of emotions was waiting there, just below the surface, ready if she decided to unleash it. She could shout and weep and wail and have Mrs. Walker thrown out, with orders never to approach the house again. She could make everyone miserable, even herself, provided she only thought about the adults involved and focused all her attention on her own sense of injury and betrayal.

But: there was a child to consider.

A child her husband loved.

Despite the envy and the bitterness of unfulfilled longing, despite the hope she still cherished for children of her own, Anne realized she couldn't separate her husband and his newborn son. It was a first step toward a family—scandal or no scandal, Anne would not break this fundamental, all-important connection. She had seen what it had cost him to lose one family member, and she would not allow him to suffer that again. But how to maintain such a connection without society learning about it? Simon could write to the boy, she supposed, as he wrote to John—but Nicholas was far too young for letters yet...

An idea was forming, pulling itself up out of the soup of emotion, observation, and instinct. Anne turned the lens of skepticism on it but found it sturdy enough. "Mrs. Walker," she said, "I wonder if I could make a proposition?"

At once the mother retrieved her child. Simon let him go, but his eyes were fixed on the boy, still marveling at his existence.

Mrs. Walker tucked Nicholas closely against her body—her smile was all politeness but the steel was back in her eyes. Anne couldn't blame her. "What kind of proposition, my lady?"

Anne had always been best when blunt, and she was true to her history now. "I wonder if you would agree to be employed as my secretary."

The silence that fell was exquisite.

Mrs. Walker had gone white. Simon goggled. Anne took a seat in a nearby chair and clasped her hands in front of her, the better to keep them from shaking. "My correspondence is taking up an increasing amount of my time and attention," she explained. "I have been thinking I should hire a secretary but have not yet had the time to make a proper search for someone suitable. You have quite an elegant hand, if memory serves—for I'm sure I've seen at least one of the letters you sent to my husband—"

"I burned them," Simon blurted. Both Anne and Mrs. Walker looked askance, and his face reddened. "Burned them all. Without reading them," he went on. "I thought it was best. I knew Canton was handling the annuity and the funds were being withdrawn from my accounts as I'd specified. I thought the only reason you were writing was to keep in contact, in case... In case I should change my mind at a later date and renew our association." He tugged at the buttons on his jacket, then stilled his hands and put them firmly behind his back. "I hope my thoughtlessness has not proved too distressing, Mrs. Walker," he said with consummate formality.

Anne could see his thoughts as clearly as if they were written on the wall behind him. She'd seen Simon this distraught and stiff-necked once before, when he'd unintentionally exposed her cousin to public shame and censure, ruining her utterly. He'd come to their home in the middle of the night, dragging his full-grown brother behind him like an errant schoolboy. Anne remembered the sickly cast of his face and the set to his jaw when he'd confessed his part in the night's events. He'd been so bluntly determined to make amends for his fault. And this was, on the face of it, so much worse: this bastard boy was not the result of a momentary slip but a product of a habit of long-standing. Proof of the father's lack of self-control and moral turpitude.

They had discussed the women in Simon's past but it had been theoretical and private at the time. Now his past was standing here in the room with them. But also here was Simon's future, in the form of young Nicholas.

Anne had no doubt which was more important to her.

It was best to clear the air so they all could move forward. "Mrs. Walker," she blurted, "are you interested in renewing your association with my husband?"

Simon let out a strangled sound and sagged against the nearest wall.

To her credit, Mrs. Walker only gaped for a moment. Then, quite carefully, she took the seat opposite Anne, chin high. "I'd rather not," she said, returning Anne's bluntness with her own. "Any such association," she spoke the word as if tasting it, "would be a strain at present, even if there were not other complications to consider."

Anne nodded, though privately she admitted to no small sense of relief. "Then I feel entirely comfortable asking you again: would you be interested in being my secretary?"

Mrs. Walker snorted, then caught herself. "May I be completely frank, my lady?" Anne ignored the ironic tone and nodded assent. "You'd think a woman with my history would be impossible to shock—but I've never once thought to have the wife of a former *parti* offer me a paid position in her household. I can't imagine why you would do such a thing."

"Can't you?" Anne returned. "It seems the best solution to a number of problems." She began ticking off reasons on her fingers, as Simon managed to push himself forward and slump onto a corner of the couch. "It will, of course, be immensely useful to have a secretary—I am selfish enough to admit that. We may have only just met, but I admire your tenacity and your poise in the face of several considerable challenges—notably my mother."

"Your mother?" Simon's voice was faint with horror.

Anne nodded. "My mother insisted on introducing herself when Mrs. Walker arrived."

"She was very gracious," Mrs. Walker hurried to add, "if a bit strong-minded."

Simon dropped his head into his hands.

Anne empathized but she was focused on her purpose and turned back to Mrs. Walker. "Most importantly," she said, her voice softening, "if you should accept the post, my husband will be able to know his son." Mrs. Walker's hands clenched on the blanket in which Nicholas was currently dozing. Anne pressed forward. "I have no intention of taking him from you. You are his mother and you are irreplaceable. But I agree with you that the boy needs his father as well."

Mrs. Walker considered this. "Would you require me to join your household? To live here?"

Anne shrugged. "That is completely up to you—I can see benefits to either arrangement."

Mrs. Walker bit her lip, thinking. "I think I will stay in my current home, then."

"Just as you like," Anne said, and stood. "I have no idea what the proper wages are for a secretary, so please name any figure you choose. Can you start tomorrow? I have an entire afternoon's writing to make up."

"Tomorrow would be fine," Mrs. Walker agreed. She stood and shook Anne's offered hand. "But for now I should probably take Nicholas home. He'll need feeding and changing." She turned back to Simon, who lurched belatedly up from his chair. "I apologize again for the shock, my lord," she murmured.

"Not at all." Simon's reply was more hapless than gracious, but Mrs. Walker only smiled and took her leave.

CHAPTER 8

$\mathcal{A}$s soon as they heard the front door shut, Simon launched himself up out of his chair, his complexion going from white to red and back again. "Your secretary! A baby! Baby! Secretary!"

"Your mistress," Anne interjected. "And your son." Perhaps she hadn't been properly gentle with her husband. She'd had an entire afternoon to absorb the news and temper her reaction; Simon had had only a matter of minutes.

He whirled on her now, his shock finding a pivot-point for its full expression. "*Your mother!*" he shouted.

Anne grimaced. "Indeed. That was...awkward."

"Awkward!" Simon collapsed helplessly onto the sofa next to Anne, legs splayed and mustache aquiver. Incoherent sounds occasionally emerged from his throat and his eyes were screwed shut as though he wished to disappear into peaceful darkness.

His wife could certainly understand that feeling.

Anne reached out and gently touched his wrist. "Can I get you anything? Tea? Brandy?"

He jerked to attention, then grasped her hand in his like a lifeline. His eyes were fierce now, desperate. "Anne, I'm so sorry," he said. "I tried to be so careful, every time we—The whole time I was with her..."

Anne smiled even though her heart twisted a little, and gripped his hands tightly. "It's no matter," she said. She knew if she said it often enough, with a strong enough conviction, it would eventually be true. "You have a beautiful son."

Simon barked a laugh. "He looks just like me."

Anne's smile faltered. "Yes."

Simon looked away. His face was back to red again. "You're a saint to forgive me such an offense," he said. "I promised you respectability in your marriage, yet within a year you're introducing *your mother* to my former mistress and my bastard child."

Anne thought about mentioning that Mrs. Pym had done the introducing but decided it was best to let it pass. "I think our reputation will survive. After all, a secretary will not be expected to mix socially with our guests or family, so her child will be easy enough for the *ton* to overlook. We'll describe her, if anyone should ask, as a gently bred but impoverished widow. Even if there are rumors, I very much doubt anybody will bring them up directly."

Simon's eyes were dark pools of worry. "But what if they do?"

"We brazen it out, of course." Anne put on what she'd come to think of as her countess voice. "My secretary's son? I beg your pardon, Lord Anyone, but clearly your lurid imagination has overwhelmed your powers of understanding. Our household is not nearly so interesting as that."

Simon sighed and brushed reverent fingertips against Anne's cheek. "I'm a little disappointed to find that you're not jealous. You always struck me as the possessive type, to be frank."

Anne turned her face into his palm. She wasn't jealous, not in the way he meant, but she couldn't bring herself to explain the true source of her envy. "Of course I am jealous," she said. "That is why I asked her if she had designs on you. But jealousy does not make me an idiot. She could only steal you from me if you wished to be stolen."

His fingers tensed and he pressed a kiss to her forehead. "But Anne," he murmured again, "what of our children? Yours and mine? Will we tell them the truth about their half brother?"

Anne had to swallow hard to untwist her throat. "I don't know," she confessed. "The question had occurred to me. I have changed my mind about it at least ten times this hour. I expect I'll change it a thousand times by tomorrow." She leaned forward and took comfort in how naturally Simon's arms curved in comfort around her shoulders. "Our own children are still waiting for us in the years to come. This child— Nicholas—is here right now. That's the most important thing."

Simon tightened his arm around her. "I don't deserve you, Anne. I'll make this up to you, I swear it."

I don't care if you deserve me, Anne thought. *Because I love you.* But she didn't say it. She merely pressed herself closer against him, as though his warmth could melt the broken pieces of her back together.

One month later, Evangeline was married. The bride wore a rose-tinted dress only a shade or two lighter than the groom's blushing face. Mrs. Pym wept copiously and Mr. Pym looked as though a great weight had been taken off his shoulders. After a luxuriant breakfast—with, Anne noted, a surfeit of light wines and champagne—the newlyweds climbed into a well-sprung carriage for the journey to the groom's country manor, where they were to spend their honeymoon.

Only as the carriage turned the corner did Anne realize how lonely she was going to be.

The season was ending. Lady Morley had already departed for Shropshire and Mrs. Bell was leaving at some point in the coming week. Others would follow suit. Simon had a few business details to see through at present, but he had talked about visiting one of his far-flung estates—a place with the imposing name of Marlston, near the wild and ancient Forest of Dean, on the opposite side of the country from the rolling hills and farms where Anne's parents had raised her and her sister and, eventually, her wilder, more rebellious cousin.

To be frank, it sounded rather lonely.

She would miss Evangeline. She missed Hecuba desperately. Anne had been too anxious on her own nuptial day to note it except in small, passing pangs, but at her sister's wedding she had been less centrally involved and she felt the full force of Hecuba's absence. For all the pleasures of a title and respectable marriage, for all the dances and dinners and even the confirmed sweetness of newly budding friendships, the loss of her cousin had become a deep and constant pulse, like a long-healed broken bone that still aches when it rains.

So it was with mixed delight and pain that she opened Hecuba's latest letter that week. Mrs. Walker was seated nearby, writing replies to the mountain of charitable requests and formal solicitations that came addressed to any countess. Anne herself handled all the personal and social correspondence—though she often wished it were the other way around. Mrs. Walker had a capable, comfortable manner and was proving tactful but ruthless when required, a combination Anne found miraculous and enviable. She'd never had the patience for real delicacy of expression, but there were already several useful turns of phrase Mrs. Walker had used that Anne was determined to steal. *I regret to decline*...followed by a thoughtful memory or compliment. *I commend your enthusiasm* was for people who were being too insistent and *I wish you all success in your efforts* looked polite enough on paper but felt like a thorough set-down.

Anne was anticipating Hecuba's usual busy tone and charming hyperbole but the content of the letter was simple, straightforward and heartbreaking.

My dear cousin, Hecuba wrote.

The effort of creating a child is apparently taxing my frail female form more than Dr. Acton thinks it should. Perhaps it's an effect of the poisonous substances I use in my colors, perhaps it's my less-than-tractable nature getting in the way of this innately female project. The good doctor has used a great many vague terms so as not to sully my poor woman's brain with abstruse medical knowledge, but the point of all his euphemisms is that I am beyond his powers as a physician and should seek examination by a specialist in the city. John is nearly out of his wits with worry as it is, so this news has put him in a state of pure irrationality. In the interest of my health and my husband's sanity, we must travel to London.

Would it be possible to visit you, or for you to visit me, even only briefly, when we arrive? I have missed you, you see. John is wonderful, but he is too much himself to be an acceptable replacement for you.

All my love, Hecuba

Anne stared so long that she jumped a little at her secretary's slight cough. "Is something the matter?" her secretary asked.

Anne nodded but couldn't quite push words through the lump in her throat. Mrs. Walker paused expectantly for a moment, then yielded to Anne's silence and resumed writing. Her brow was smooth, her hand steady so that no errant drops of ink marred the white margin of the paper. Her gown, as usual, was elegantly simple with carefully tailored lines that accented the perfection of her figure. Anne thought that if a stranger saw them now, he would assume Mrs. Walker was the countess and Anne was the secretary.

In her earlier life, Anne had often considered what might happen to her should she fail to marry well or if her family were financially as well as socially ruined. A succession of poor harvests or a sudden taste for gambling could easily wipe out her father's meager fortune. Anne had fretted over both possibilities, deep in the privacy of the night, and had tried to plan against them. She would have been relieved to be some titled lady's secretary: it was useful work and not unpleasant. Governesshood had loomed, stern and joyless, in her possible futures. Paid companionship, as well, though all her female relatives lived in straitened circumstances and thus were not likely to provide her with a stipend for her support. When she'd occasionally voiced such worries to her cousin, Hecuba had only laughed and promised to endow her with thousands when she was rich, in some glittering future. Anne had found even this flimsy promise soothing.

And now it was Hecuba who was asking for comfort. "Is it very frightening?" Anne blurted to Mrs. Walker. "Expecting a child, I mean."

The secretary leaned back and folded her hands in her lap. She appeared relaxed enough but Anne could see how her knuckles whitened at the tightness of her grip. "Very," she said at last. "I suffered a miscarriage many years ago, so I had some experience with the early stages, but it only made everything worse. I feared the same thing might happen with Nicholas—but at the same time it would make things so much simpler if I didn't have to worry about a child. Every day seemed to last for months, until suddenly they were putting my newborn son into my arms." A ghostly smile washed over her and was just as quickly gone. "It was like the sun breaking through clouds."

Anne bit her lip hard. She only spoke when she had herself well in hand. "Was it...was it a very difficult birth?"

Mrs. Walker's blue eyes had gone bright and hard again, as they did whenever she felt the need to protect herself. "I couldn't tell you," she said. "They tell me it wasn't but it seemed difficult enough when I was lying in that bed for two straight days and nights, feeling as though I were being slowly torn in half. The midwife's assistant was drunk and nearly dropped the baby, in the end." Anne's hands clenched at that, Hecuba's letter crumpling and cracking beneath her fingers. Mrs. Walker's expression was resigned. "Is there something you have to tell me, my lady?"

For one shameful moment Anne wished she could say yes. That she had conceived. She knew the prospect of a legitimate heir would make Mrs. Walker uneasy. The other woman didn't trust her yet, not in matters as important her own and her son's future. Anne had no interest in setting up a rivalry between herself and the former courtesan, or between her child and any legitimate offspring Anne might have with Simon, but she still yearned for children of her own. A family—one that loved and protected one another. Nicholas could still be a part of that family, but this was not the moment to confess all her hopes in that direction. "It's my cousin," she said instead. "Simon's brother's wife. She is expecting, and apparently the situation is becoming...a cause for concern. The doctor is quite troubled."

Mrs. Walker's expression didn't change but Anne noticed the line of her shoulders soften. "I'm sorry," the secretary murmured. "Is there anything I can do?"

"No, but I thank you." Anne pressed the letter flat on the writing-desk, trying to smooth out all the wrinkles in the paper. Words jumped out at her like inky darts: *beg, worry, love.* She passed a finger over that last one, written out in Hecuba's careful chemist's hand.

Anne knew everyone would advise against the visit. Anne's mother thought Hecuba a lost cause, a stain on the family name. And pleasant though they were, both Lady Morley and Mrs. Bell would counsel her to err on the side of social propriety. Simon...

Well, Simon might think differently.

Simon might miss John as much as Anne missed Hecuba.

She pushed all the other notes and invitations aside and rose to her feet. "If you'll pardon me a moment," she said to Mrs. Walker, "there's something I need to ask my husband about."

Babies, Simon had decided, were disgusting little creatures. There always seemed to be something oozing, dripping or leaking out of them from one end or, worse, the other. Only this afternoon, Nicholas and his various effluvia had ruined Simon's gloves, cuffs, cravat, waistcoat, and shirtfront—all in less than an hour, and all from a child who lacked even the ability to hold up his own wobbly, soft, babyish head.

Clearly the boy was a prodigy.

He was also providing Simon this afternoon with a much-needed hiatus from all the work that went into maintaining the earldom. Tenant disputes, cottage repair, early harvest preparations by his several stewards, a few financial endeavors he had helped to fund and wished to personally track the progress of... He told himself it was noble and necessary, that he'd been raised and trained and educated so as to be the strong and lauded head of this empire in miniature, but every so often his soul rose up and chafed beneath a burden he hadn't selected for himself.

Well, he hadn't chosen Nicholas either, but something about the process of caring for his son an hour or two a week—of soothing, watching, entertaining, cossetting and withstanding the grumpy presence of a wordlessly wailing infant—seemed to untie something inside Simon, to lessen the general sense of weight and tension he seemed to have been carrying around for years. That relief was worth any number of new shirts and linens.

A soft knock at the study door heralded his countess, looking particularly fetching in a deep-blue gown. Simon hoisted his son up in the air and smiled at his wife. "Is Mrs. Walker leaving so soon?" he asked. She shook her head. Something tight in her expression sobered him up and sent away the last few wisps of relaxed good feeling. "What is the matter?"

When Anne straightened her shoulders and lifted her chin, he knew it was going to be something significant. "I'm thinking of having John and Hecuba to stay with us," she said.

Her voice was calm but the force of her words nearly laid him out flat. Simon tucked the baby more securely into the crook of his arm. Anne was waiting for his response, her eyes unnaturally bright and her shoulders set in expectation of a fight. He wasn't going to give it to her. "Why?" he asked gently.

"Because they've asked," Anne said. "Because they're family, and I miss her, and I'll bet you miss your brother." She took a breath that had a bit of a shudder at the end, and it was only then that Simon became truly alarmed. "Because Hecuba's health is suffering and they need to consult a specialist here in London."

"Bloody hell." Anne didn't flinch at all at the language. Simon sat down heavily in a well-stuffed chair, Nicholas twisting at the change in position then relaxing again against his father's torso.

"It's the end of the season," Anne hurried to say. "Most people have left town already and the few who remain are entertaining far less frequently. So it's entirely possible that they will come, Hecuba will have the baby and they'll leave again before anybody knows they've been."

The earl looked at his wife. "But those few still might find out. And if they find out, they will talk."

She nodded.

He pressed forward, hating himself a little for it. "They won't be kind. This won't be as easy as when you hired Mrs. Walker." As if at the mention of his mother, the baby waved a fist in the air and negligently rammed it into Simon's chest. The earl gripped the boy's hands together loosely in one of his. "You might be ruined all over again," he said.

"*We* might be a little ruined, yes." Anne took another long, shuddering breath, then let it out again. "I've thought of that," she said. "But I've been thinking about other things lately as well. I've been missing Hecuba dreadfully—you can't grow up with someone like a sister, then rest easy when they're cut out of your life. It's as if I've lost an arm and I keep trying to reach out with a hand that no longer exists."

Simon's gut twisted at this. He'd done everything he could to make her happy—the marriage, the gowns, the pleasuring—and he knew she appreciated all of it, but it wasn't enough to counter the other hurts in her life. Hurts that he knew he'd helped to create in one moment of thoughtlessness. John and Hecuba between them might have forged the blade that had wounded Anne, but Simon had helped them sharpen it.

And now even the respectability he'd offered in recompense would be taken away from her, all because she was loving and loyal and missed her cousin. Titled tongues would wag and the frequency and number of invitations would dwindle.

Anne would end up lonely again.

He'd loved seeing her spread her wings in the rarified air of high society. He couldn't bear the thought that the same people who'd taken such delight in her company would cast her aside on account of a year-old scandal—but he knew that some would. There was a powerful element of the *ton* that had erected an altar to a limited vision of morality and correctness, and they would gleefully tear down anyone who visibly offended that ideal. John and Hecuba's affair had stunned all of London even before she went into trade as a colorist, and anyone publicly associated with them would be tarred with the same brush. Everything Anne had worked for, before and after her marriage, would be erased and forgotten like frost in summer.

At the same time, how could he refuse? Hecuba's health must take priority. Anne would never forgive him if he left family to suffer when he could have done something to help. "Of course they can stay with us," he said.

Simon would simply have to find a way to make it all up to her.

Anne's smile was a bonfire of relief. "Thank you," she said.

The earl didn't have time to reply, as Nicholas had woken up and embarked upon one of his usual post-nap grumpy periods. Simon was always surprised that so tiny a mouth could emit so forceful a noise. Anne gave him a sympathetic look and returned to the parlor, eager to write to Hecuba with a positive reply.

Two more naps, one bath—given by the maid but supervised by the earl—and one hour later, Mrs. Walker and Nicholas returned to their own quiet home.

Simon was left in his study, thinking hard about his wife.

CHAPTER 9

*B*y the end of that night, Simon had a solution—and with it, a new priority.

He was going to give Anne the family she'd always wanted.

He couldn't fix his past mistakes and he didn't have a tight-knit circle of friends to surround her with and help to lessen her isolation. But he could give her children. Three or four little ones for her to raise, to protect, to love, to spoil with all the thoughts and plans and affection she had been storing up for years. He'd seen how she looked at Nicholas, with that combination of despair and hunger. She'd married him to get children and it was high time he gave her what she wanted.

So he entered her bedroom that night brimful of determination. They hadn't fucked each other since the night her courses had started—but that had been over a week ago. Surely she would be ready for him again.

Anne was wrapped in a dressing gown and curled up in a chair, staring at the fire. The furniture in the countess's bedroom was daintier than in the earl's, with slender legs and elaborate scrollwork from the previous century. Anne herself looked equally fragile, and all Simon's mustered heartiness vanished in a sudden rush of worry. "What's wrong?"

She started a little and whipped her head around, then relaxed when she saw who it was who had spoken. "I was just thinking."

There wasn't another chair, so Simon sat on the rug at her feet. This was getting to be a habit, he reflected, but then she threaded her fingers into his hair and he leaned back against her legs with a contented sigh. "Thinking about what?" he asked.

"The chasm between the ideal countess and my own interpretation of the role," she replied. "I feel as if you wanted Sarah Siddons but you married Nell Gwynn."

"So long as some king doesn't steal you from me." Simon laughed, but when he looked up Anne's smile was crooked, a thorn directed inwardly. He sobered at once. "How are you not the ideal countess?" he asked.

"So many ways," she sighed. "I'm suspicious and petulant, too frank at times and too shy at others. I wasn't raised in the *ton*, so its secret rules and manners look awkward and unnatural on me. I should either light up a room with gaiety when I enter it, or else I should bring a soothing aura of perfect tranquility and peace. And I haven't even been wifely enough to give you an heir yet." Her fingers in his hair shifted slightly. "There are countless reasons why you should regret ever marrying me."

"I don't, though," Simon said. The fingers went still in surprise. "I think it's the best thing that's ever happened to me." He gazed steadily up at her at her, watching the firelight pool in her dark eyes. "All those society misses, as precious and delicate and breakable as porcelain? I felt oafish, a lumbering ox beside them. And if the ox was considered a superior sort of beast, it was only because he came draped in a title and hauling a fortune behind him. I certainly never felt I could attach anyone on my personal charms alone." He caught her hand in his and held it as tightly as he dared. "I didn't know what I was looking for until you offered it—someone strong, someone honest, someone who would get exasperated and attack problems rather than covering them with smiles and lace and pretending they didn't exist." He twined his fingers with hers, turning their joined hands over in the warm light from the fire. "I never quite lived up to my father's expectations for the ideal earl: why should my countess be more conventional than myself?"

She seized both his hands in hers, turning fierce. "Your father did you a great disservice," she said. "He made a pattern in his mind and punished you for not fitting it. It's not real—but you are. You are brimming with the best kind of honor and respect, no matter what you think about feeling like an ox, and if he couldn't love you for yourself, then he didn't deserve such a fine, stalwart man as his son. But he's gone and his shadow need not darken this house or your heart any longer. From now on, you must wear the title as a man who deserves it, who embodies nobility." She licked her lips, blushing slightly. "Who is loved very much by his countess."

Simon couldn't move, couldn't speak, couldn't breathe. His heart had shattered perfectly, like a wineglass at the highest note of the aria, and the rest of him was left shaking, vibrant and stunned. Anne's blush deepened and she freed one hand to trace along his jawline, so tenderly.

Her touch released him. Frantically he pulled her down from the chair, then rolled her beneath him. Silk and brocade filled his hands as he tugged at her garments, his mouth hot on the soft skin of her neck. She gasped into his ear and managed to undo the tie of his robe. Red wool billowed around them. Simon yanked the fabric out from between their bodies just as Anne shifted her legs and the skirts of her dressing gown parted. She was entirely naked beneath, nothing but skin and scent and a patch of dark, curling hair that drew him in like a lodestone.

God, he would never get tired of the sounds she made when his mouth was on her. He worked at her like a man starved, until she was sopping wet and flushed bright pink and the fine, savory scent of her filled his nose and lingered on his eager tongue. His mouth moved to her breast and his fingers plunged inside her as she hissed and arched up, clutching his shoulders and demanding more in that stern voice that sparked against him like steel on flint. When his fingers were thoroughly soaked in her wetness she gasped and spread her thighs—he took the hint and slammed his cock deep into her cunt.

Anne swore, a low string of profanity that only spurred Simon on. He sped up, thrusting as hard as he could while his wife writhed beneath him and dug her fingernails into the meat of his shoulder. "Harder," she demanded, and he tried to comply but the angle was tricky and his robe kept tangling beneath his knees and his hands and setting him off-kilter.

With a growl, he slid out of her and tore the robe from his shoulders. Anne slipped out of her dressing gown and turned her back to him, bending at the waist and pushing her knees wide, spreading herself as open as she could get. Within seconds Simon was back inside her, her back against his chest, one hand flat on the floor supporting his weight while the other moved impulsively along the length of her body, hip to breast to shoulder. All the while Simon pounded into her as hard as he dared, as she moaned encouragement and slid one hand between her legs to stroke her clitoris while he fucked her. When she finally shook and came, her whole body bowed beneath him and her cunt clenched hard around his thrusting cock. Simon gasped for a desperate breath and flooded her, pressing as deep as he could, blinded and choked by the force of his climax.

Together they collapsed onto their sides among the pile of discarded clothing. Anne's shoulders heaved against his chest while she fought to steady her breath. Simon wrapped one arm around her waist and nestled his face into the damp crook of her neck. "My mother once told me that children happened when two people loved each other more than could be contained by only two hearts," he said. Anne's breath caught, and Simon's lips curved briefly against her warm skin. "If that were true," he went on, "we'd have a dozen children by now."

She laughed and wriggled around to face him. "You are deeply sentimental for an ox," she said, but her smile banished any possible hurt from the term.

OLIVIA WAITE

"And you are delightfully lustful for a countess," he replied with a grin, then kissed away her half-serious protests. "My countess."

~

Hecuba arrived in London one week after Anne's invitation. It was nearly tea and Anne and Mrs. Walker were once again at work in the parlor, while Simon and Nicholas were doing whatever secret masculine things one did in an earl's study. Phillips came in with the barest hint of a smile, which on him was the equivalent of an ear-to-ear grin. "The Honorable Mr. and Mrs. John Rushmore," he intoned.

Anne rose to her feet as Hecuba waddled past the butler and opened her arms wide to embrace her cousin. She was wider of face and enormously rounded of belly, but her hair was as wild and red as ever and her eyes glowed with the same mischievous light. "I'd swear that coach travel is as bad for the digestion as sea-journeys," she said. "Not that John's ever taken me to sea."

"You'd lead a mutiny by the end of the first week," her husband returned.

Hecuba pointedly ignored him. "Let me just visit my room and be thoroughly sick for a moment, then I'll be much better company," she said. Anne distinctly heard Mrs. Walker turn a laugh into a cough behind her. Hecuba caught it, winked at the secretary and trundled out of the room as Phillips hurried to intercept and show her to the bedroom that had been readied for her.

Her husband watched her leave with a perfect mixture of admiration and concern. "Thank you again for letting us come to stay," he said, turning back to Anne. He was taller than his older brother and a bit blonder, as though he'd been ever so slightly gilded. During her first weeks in London, Anne had seen him gleaming at dinners and gliding across the parquet floors of society ballrooms, and she'd thought him unassailably out of her

86

reach. Even when she'd talked to him, he'd felt as aloof as a mountain peak. Strange to think he was now her brother-in-law and a social pariah, a tradesman who sold paints with his scandalous wife out of an ivy-covered cottage in the country. Country life apparently agreed with him—his clothes had lost some of their tailored precision but he had an indefinable aura of contentment that made him even more charming than before. The gold was harvest-gold now, not rococo.

He turned the full force of his charm on Mrs. Walker and bowed politely. "I beg the honor of an introduction to your friend," he said—then froze, the smile congealing on his face.

The secretary clasped her hands demurely in front of her. "I believe we have met before, Mr. Rushmore."

Anne was certain she spoke the truth. John looked as though he wanted to run from the room and join his wife in being spectacularly ill. Anne took a deep breath and put on her best countess manners. "Mrs. Walker has lately become my secretary, Mr. Rushmore," she said. "She is a great help to me."

"Is she really?" he murmured, then went scarlet. "How...pleasant to see you again, madam." Fiona said nothing— really, what could she say?—and John visibly sought for some polite way out of the mess he'd found himself in.

Anne was seized by a gleeful sense of vengeance and was disinclined to explain. John Rushmore had made her life profoundly unpleasant not that many months ago. Let him have a few uncomfortable moments of his own, wondering why his brother's mistress was now assistant to his wife. But she couldn't get any work done with him gaping like a hooked fish either. "I believe Simon is in the study, sir, if you'd like to look for him there."

"Yes—yes, of course," he stammered. "That would be excellent." He bowed—most correctly, Anne had to give him that —and left the room at very nearly a run.

Anne turned back to Mrs. Walker, whose cheeks were scarlet with an embarrassment her face otherwise refused to admit.

Anne's viciousness slid effortlessly into protectiveness. Impulsively, she grabbed the other woman's hand. "I want you to let me know if he makes things difficult for you," she said. "This is not his house any longer—it's mine, and you have just as much right to be here as the Honorable John Rushmore does."

Mrs. Walker's eyes narrowed even as her hands tightened around Anne's. "Why are you so kind to me?" she asked. It was the sharpest tone Anne had ever heard her use. "What could you possibly gain by it?"

The countess blinked. "What could I possibly gain by being cruel to you?" Anne countered.

"Satisfaction," Mrs. Walker returned. "Retribution. A little of your own back, as the saying goes." She dropped Anne's hands and turned away, wrapping her arms around her waist and taking one long breath after another. "My apologies, my lady. Sometimes I let my tongue get the better of me."

So her secretary wasn't always so polite and perfect. Inwardly, Anne felt some deeply buried tension uncoil—just a little bit, but enough. "Shall I tell you why I find you so interesting, Mrs. Walker?" she asked.

The blonde's head lifted and, with a piercing glance, she nodded.

"You seem so at ease—even just now, when you claim you lost control a little. You were indignant, perhaps, but righteously so." She worried a little at the lace on her cuff, then lifted her eyes again. "I can never pretend to be anything but myself," Anne admitted. "I can't hide my thoughts, I can't offer polite compliments if I don't believe them. I have strange fixations that seem to happen without my willing them—for instance, I have always wanted a large family of my own, even when there seemed no hope that I would ever get one, because my prospects for a good marriage were as far above me as the stars in the heavens. Now here I am, with a husband and a title and no concrete idea how to behave with regard to either." Mrs. Walker paled and began to protest, and Anne held up a hand. "No, I'm not asking for your help with Simon— we're doing quite well, all things considered. But being titled is not something I ever foresaw. People expect things of a countess they'd never expect from a mere miss. I feel like a pretender to the throne, or a foreigner who's just learned the language being asked to perform Shakespeare. But you know something of how this world works, Mrs. Walker—you know the codes and the unwritten rules. You are comfortable moving between registers. It's a useful trait in a secretary." She paused, then gathered her courage and spoke the final thought. "It would be a marvelous trait in a friend."

Mrs. Walker slowly sat down in a nearby chair, hands wrapped around the arms, her wary expression easing into thoughtfulness. "I don't have many friends," she said at length. "My profession did not make it easy to cultivate them. I knew many other women and many men, but I found it exceedingly difficult to trust them with any but the shallowest emotions." She quirked her lips a little. "Perhaps it has made me more guarded than I ought to be, now that I come to think about it."

Anne dared a smile in return. "I would trade some of your guardedness for some of my candor any day."

Mrs. Walker looked away and her hands subsided into their usual placid folds. "It just seemed so strange that you would defend me against your own brother-in-law. Especially since you are related to him twice over by marriage."

Anne leaned forward. "But surely you know the story?"

Mrs. Walker's eyes kindled with interest as she shook her head.

Anne lowered her voice, not so much out of fear of being overheard as to better dramatize the tale. "John and Hecuba met in the middle of the night when she broke into this very house. She was hoping to steal back some paintings that should have been hers by right of inheritance. John caught her, but instead of alerting the authorities he proposed a bargain: she could take one painting for every portrait of her she let him paint. It all had to happen at night, in secret and by candlelight, so it wasn't long before things...progressed. All while they pretended barely to know each other in front of society and their families." Anne had been close enough to Hecuba to suspect something at the time, but she'd had no idea of the full scope of the affair until it had been too late. "They nearly got away with it—until Simon found his brother's paintings and decided to display them at a party for John's fast social set. Including, to John's horror, a nude. Painted from memory, without Hecuba's knowledge."

"Was she recognizable?" Anne nodded. Mrs. Walker blanched. "She must have been furious."

"Everyone was—Hecuba, Simon, my father. Harsh words were exchanged. Fists were thrown. My father and Simon were adamant that John would have to marry her. Hecuba was equally adamant that she wouldn't have him, not after such a betrayal. Father threatened to throw her out if she didn't. And John..." Anne could still taste the bitterness of that night whenever she recalled it. "John just stood there, useless and silent, looking as though he were about to be sick."

"But he did marry her," Mrs. Walker said.

"He didn't," Anne replied. "Not for another month. Not until Hecuba had decided to forgive him. Not until she sneaked back here to propose. If he hadn't looked so blissful during the ceremony I'd have worried she bullied him into it." Mrs. Walker chuckled. "So you see," Anne finished, "I have very little cause to trust John Rushmore. Even if he has been an appallingly thoughtful husband to Hecuba. Maybe I'll forgive him fully after a decade or so of good behavior."

"I'd make it two decades if I were you," said Mrs. Walker, with a bit of that edge resurfacing in her tone. "She could have been put out on the street while he was dithering about feeling sorry for himself. I've known many fathers do as much with far less cause—to their own daughters, much less an orphaned cousin." She avoided Anne's curious gaze, her lips pressing together. "You're lucky to have such a father, so devoted to you and your protection."

Anne was suddenly very tired. She'd forgotten the feeling of those horrible days— the weight of the silence, the palpable tension in the air, heavy with words that went unspoken but not unfelt. She'd felt as though her very body and not merely the household were being slowly but inexorably drawn and quartered. "He would have done it," she said softly. "My father would have thrown her out that very night, into the darkest gutter, with only the clothes on her back—except I threatened to go with her. And that would have upset my mother, who would have wailed for years. My father values his peace, you see."

"I see," Mrs. Walker said. Her fingers clenched once, then relaxed again. "Family hurts run the deepest," she said eventually.

Anne nodded. "That's part of why I married Simon," she said. "Because even as furious as he was, he never once forgot John was his brother." She straightened her spine and shook off the miasma of old hurts. They had no place in her current life. "Some of us are not lucky in the families we're born into," she said. "Sometimes we have to build our own families, and to build them better, on more solid foundations."

Mrs. Walker's smile grew and grew, lighting up the whole room, and Anne could suddenly see why she had been successful as a courtesan. "Despite mistakes," Mrs. Walker said. "Despite illegitimacy. Despite even a past brimful of whoredom."

Anne flushed. "Not a gentle word, Mrs. Walker."

"Not a gentle life," the woman replied gently, and held out one hand. "And please, call me Fiona."

Anne's heart gave a leap within her and she took the offered hand gladly. "Then you must call me Anne."

"Of course," Fiona replied.

Anne turned back to her letters, feeling as though a fountain of warmth were overflowing the bounds of her heart. It wasn't just young Nicholas who was part of the new family they were gathering around them—there was plenty of room for Nicholas' mother too. And Hecuba.

And maybe, in some rosy future, there would even be room for John Rushmore.

But she hoped to make him suffer a little first.

~

Upstairs, Simon was using the paintings in his study to try to teach Nicholas about colors. "Red," he said, enunciating carefully and pointing to the bold brushstrokes of the sunset. "Orange. Blue."

He turned at a soft knock behind him and saw his brother standing in the doorway, flesh and blood and breath and everything. Simon wanted to laugh or cheer or cry or all three at once, and the roil of emotions rose up in his throat and choked him. He hadn't realized how much he'd missed his brother's presence—both the charming ne'er-do-well and the brooding artist sides of him. "Come in!" he said with a grin so wide it made his face ache. "I've finally found someone who likes these odd paintings of yours." It was an old joke, nearly worn out with use, but his heart was too full for novelty .

John didn't laugh. John, in fact, looked furious. "What is Fiona Walker doing in your front parlor?" he demanded.

Simon couldn't immediately follow this change in topic. "What?"

John shut the door behind him and strode forward, his voice low and urgent. "What—is your *mistress*—doing downstairs—with your *wife*?"

The earl gaped. This was his easy-going, devil-may-care brother? The man who'd once held comfortable week-long debauches in the country and memorable night-long orgies in this very house? Who'd enjoyed tweaking society's nose for as long as he'd been alive, from his childish pranks to his roguish flirtations to the artistic aspirations that he clung to despite their parents' and the *ton*'s disapproval?

Nicholas gave a dissatisfied yawp.

John's gaze was dragged downward and the flush bled out of his face. "Bloody hell," he whispered.

Not for the first time, Simon tamped down a flash of regret that his illegitimate son bore so strong a resemblance to his father. There would be many moments like this in the future, when his relationship to Nicholas would be impossible to hide from even a casual observer. The looming exasperation made his reply sharper than he intended. "There's no need to be so dramatic," he said. "I know quite well this is not the first bastard among your acquaintance."

"Perhaps not," John shot back, "but it's the first one I'm related to. Simon, what the hell are you thinking to bring your mistress and her son so openly into your house?"

Simon bit back a snappish reply. He'd reacted in much the same way himself on the day he'd first met Nicholas. "Mrs. Walker is not my mistress," he said, his voice clipped. "We parted amicably some months before Anne and I were married. I didn't even know about the boy until recently—she'd written to me about him, but I never read the notes. That chapter of my life was over, though I can see now how ridiculous that sounds." John's mouth was hanging wide open at this point, to Simon's secret pleasure. He forged on ruthlessly. "Well, Mrs. Walker showed up on the doorstep one day, determined to see me and tell me about my son. I wasn't home. My wife, however, was. She took a liking to Fiona and insisted on hiring her as her secretary. It seems to be working very well, and nobody is more surprised and relieved than myself."

"How very pleasant for you all," John shot back. The sheer amount of venom in his tone would have choked even the most poisonous Egyptian adder. "How forgiving of your wife to overlook such a moral failure. How gracious of you to give your whore a way to earn an honest living."

Every drop of blood in Simon's body congealed, then petrified. He wasn't a man any longer—he was a statue, an iced-over fountain with water-pipes instead of veins and nothing but cold stone where his heart should be. His face felt stiff and heavy, barely moving when he spoke. "Hecuba is here at my wife's request," he said. "Her health will not be jeopardized. But we have no need for you, if this is the kind of tone you will set for your visit. Luckily, you have not yet had time to unpack your things, so it will be no trouble for you to leave at once and find some comfortable gutter into which to vomit up any other such vile opinions."

Nicholas began to fuss again. Simon turned back to the painting and held his son high enough for baby eyes to see the bright splashes and slashes of color on the canvas. The boy calmed at once. Simon wished his own anger could be as easily soothed. The ice inside was cracking now, blasted away by a fury he didn't understand and could barely keep leashed. He knew what he would hear next—footsteps and a door clicking shut with a sound like a coffin-lid closing.

Instead John began to speak, his voice as soft as a snowflake. "What I don't understand is how Mrs. Walker came to be more important to you than your own brother. Why you would risk social outcry on her behalf…but not on mine."

The brushstrokes in the sunset painting were already indistinct and slapdash but they blurred further as tears pooled in Simon's vision. He gritted his teeth and hung on to the dying embers of his rage. "We risk very little by employing Mrs. Walker. She does not live in this house and she does not join us at social events. What she asks of us is a trifle. Your recklessness nearly destroyed the hopes of an entire family—my wife's family and yours. I bear some responsibility for that, I will admit." This next part very nearly stuck in his throat but he forced it out. "Father told me never to regret doing what is correct. And so our family split apart because we had both erred in society's eyes. But there is propriety and then there is doing what is right. It was not right for you and me to abandon each other. I know that now, and since marrying Anne I have tried to live by better principles. For her sake even more than my own."

For a time there was only the crackling of the fire and the occasional happy noise of a distracted infant. Simon held Nicholas up to the painting and waited for his brother to say something, anything in response.

Behind the earl, John cleared his throat. "What is it you're doing with the boy?"

Simon wanted to shout with joy and wrap his arms around his brother. Instead he merely arched an eyebrow. "Your nephew apparently shares your eye for experimental artwork depicting indeterminate subjects."

"That's a sunset," John responded, his contrarian instincts reasserting themselves.

"It's a mess," Simon retorted.

"That baby has a better eye than you do." With a groan, he slumped heavily into the scratched leather armchair by the hearth. "I'm banished for less than a year and you turn incorrigible on me."

"Upset that your older brother has outstripped your shocking reputation?" Simon needled.

"I have no reputation," John said with a laugh that almost equaled his usual breezy tone. "I'm a mere tradesman now, and scandals are bad for business." His hands plucked at a tear in the leather. "I've missed you," he said. "The country can be quite lonely, even with Hecuba keeping everyone busy and distracted."

"Well, you're here now, aren't you?" Simon said gruffly, then plunked his giggling son into his uncle's hastily lifted arms. "Here —tell your nephew something about this painting that I don't know." John goggled at him, then Nicholas, then Simon again. Simon only shrugged, fighting off the absurd warmth that was filling his chest. "If he's going to stare at art, he might as well start learning what to look for."

CHAPTER 10

*H*ecuba never came back down that first afternoon. Anne checked with the maids and found that she'd been casting up her accounts fairly regularly, but seemed to be bearing it with a wry and self-deprecating chagrin. John Rushmore—who had come down to dinner in a far better temper than when Anne had last seen him—told her that their physician had Hecuba on bed rest, which she adamantly resisted as often as she could. "He was concerned that she should be past the worst of the illness by now," he said.

"Motherhood is an illness?" Anne had quipped.

John had merely smiled wanly. "You'd be surprised."

He'd bidden farewell to Fiona with enough grace to make up for his earlier brusque reception and seemed to be on perfectly jovial terms with Simon. They teased and joked all through dinner, telling Anne stories from their childhood, trying to outdo each other with embarrassing adventures and boyish pranks. The next morning they left early in search of some manly entertainment or other—races or horse auctions or something like that, Anne wasn't sure—and Anne went about her correspondence. Letters were longer in the summer, with friends farther away, but the press of impersonal missives had eased and

Fiona was mostly able to read, or to tend to whatever part of Nicholas needed feeding, cleaning or comforting.

Hecuba lumbered in an hour later, one hand on her back, skirts billowing around her enlarged form. Her eyes were as bright with mischief as ever, but close observation showed dark circles beneath them and a too-wan complexion. She lowered herself to the sofa with a sigh of relief.

Anne's pen skittered across the paper as she tried to finish her letter to Lady Morley. "Aren't you supposed to be on bed rest?" she said.

Her cousin huffed. "You're as bad as John."

Anne turned the paper over and began a second page. "John is worried about you."

"Then he should have had this baby himself." Fiona smothered a laugh, drawing Hecuba's attention. "Hello," she said, and offered one hand, as gracefully as a queen. "I'm Hecuba Rushmore."

Fiona walked over and grasped her hand. "Fiona Walker," she said. "Secretary to the Countess of Underwood."

Hecuba cocked her head at Anne. "So strange to think of you with a title," she said. "Countess of Underwood has such a patrician ring to it."

"Don't make too much fun," Anne returned. "John's first in the line of succession— if something were to happen to Simon, you'd be a countess quicker than you could say '*noblesse oblige*'."

"You'd be Dowager Countess then, so at least I'd have company." Hecuba twisted her shoulders and wormed her way lower into the sofa cushions. "You really ought to get yourself a real heir so I wouldn't have to worry about it. That one doesn't count," she said, with a wave at Nicholas.

Anne stopped writing mid-word and Fiona went utterly still.

Hecuba smiled ruefully. "John told me," she said. "I think he wanted to warn me, in case I would go all shocked and sputtery as he apparently did." She folded her hands over her belly. "I think he forgets how disreputable our own introductions were."

She delivered this line with a carefully casual tone—a hunter setting bait in a trap.

Anne snorted. "I already told Fiona the whole story."

Hecuba's disappointment was so evident that Fiona laughed out loud. Anne's cousin huffed again and pushed a strand of red hair out of her eyes. "I had planned that story to last at least half an hour," she complained. "It's impossible to fill time when one is an invalid. There's only so many Gothic novels one can read with any interest. And here I don't even have the option of sneaking out to the workshop when John's away."

Anne's mouth dropped open. She had not forgotten the odors, acids and gases that so often resulted from Hecuba's pigment recipes and experiments. She'd lost more pairs of gloves over the years to her cousin's paint-stained fingers than she cared to remember. "Hecuba, are you telling me that you've been working with those vile toxins of yours while you're with child?"

Her cousin's mouth turned down at the corners. "I haven't touched anything dangerous. Mostly I've been grinding ore and preparing samples for when I am at liberty to work again. John doesn't have the knack for the more complicated recipes, and some of our stocks are beginning to run low. Besides, it's probably no worse for me than this fetid London air." She met Anne's scowl with one of her own. "I have never been so bored in my life. If this child doesn't decide to arrive soon, I may just shove my hand up there and yank him out myself."

Now Anne was truly shocked. Hecuba was in the habit of saying things just to be provoking, but she'd never sounded so...*violent* before.

Fiona, however, only laughed. "In my last weeks, instead of lullabies, I walked around whispering 'Get out, get out, get out' to Nicholas in the womb."

"Oh!" Hecuba chortled. "Did your ankles swell up like mine have?" She kicked one foot free of her skirts—to Anne's horror, her foot and calf were so distended as to be unrecognizable, swollen and elephantine. "My body has betrayed me," she proclaimed, with evident feeling. "I'm not sure it will ever go back to its former size and shape. I should be mortified by how I look but I'm too uncomfortable to care."

Fiona only laughed at this as well. "Just you wait until your time arrives. I thought I lacked the capacity to be embarrassed in front of strangers—one requires that in my former profession—but childbirth has a way of obliterating any form of shame and replacing it with equal parts rage and exhaustion."

They continued this line of conversation for some time. Swellings, aches, errant baby fists and feet, odors, leaks, whip-quick changes of mood. Anne, aghast, turned back to her letters, but her eyes could barely focus on the swirls of ink on the page.

Motherhood sounded *terrible*. Uncomfortable at the best of times and agonizing at the worst. Fiona and Hecuba were clearly reveling in the horror, trying to outdo each other in pain and suffering. There was no sense of the nobility of maternity, of the abiding tenderness of motherly affection, of the moral solace of having done one's duty as a woman and as a wife. Instead there was this messy, frustrating, potentially fatal transformation into something alien and unrecognizable. They sounded less like mothers and more like soldiers comparing wounds from a shared campaign.

And then Fiona handed Nicholas to Hecuba, who bounced him up and down on his fat baby legs, and they grinned so widely at each other that Anne's face ached in envy .

She hastily folded up her latest missive and pushed herself up from the desk. "I'm going to give this to Phillips," she said, and tried to walk out as though she weren't fleeing from the room.

The marble foyer was cooler than the parlor, with no windows letting in the unusually harsh summer sun. Phillips was nowhere to be seen—probably in the kitchens speaking with the cook—but he'd only been a pretext for escape. Anne wrapped her arms around herself and tried to breathe. Every day since her marriage she'd woken up and wondered if she and Simon had already conceived or if this was the day it would happen. She'd thought it would be a sweet, sharp pleasure, something like the first bloom of a spring crocus after a long and hopeless winter. Something she would have to discover through careful attention.

But Anne hadn't conceived, not if Hecuba and Fiona's stories were any guide. Apparently babies didn't only kick and scream when they were born, but from the moment of conception onward. If she were expecting, she would know it. She couldn't help knowing it—her body would be shouting it from every atom.

But there was no shouting. There wasn't even a whisper, not the least little twinge of bone or pull of muscle. Her stomach was unroiled. Her ankles were maiden-slender. Her sleep at night was untroubled by the constant need to use the privy. She was an absolute paragon of health.

And she hated it.

Why, if such suffering was what she had to look forward to, did she still envy the two mothers all their aches and troubles? She'd never been the type for martyrdom. Indeed she trembled even now, imagining her body growing and filling and stretching under its own mysterious power, ignoring any attempt at or need for control.

But simply learning about the pain didn't do anything to lessen her desire for children. It still nestled just below her breastbone, burrowed deep and curled around itself like a fox in winter.

There would be pain, then.

But it would be worth it.

She remembered the look she caught occasionally on Fiona's face when she looked at Nicholas. Some mixture of exasperation, affection and profound wonder.

Anne wanted to feel what lay beneath that look. She wanted to care about someone else that much, that quickly, that deeply. She wanted to see what it felt like when her heart opened wide enough to put someone else first, always.

You couldn't have that kind of growth without sacrifice.

She took one last breath to steady herself, left her letter on the tray for Phillips and returned to the parlor.

That night, when she entered Simon's bedroom, Anne was ready.

More than ready, really. Determined. Prepared. Outfitted in her mind like a general advancing toward the enemy.

Her husband was just removing his cravat. He'd gotten into the habit of dispensing with a valet in the evenings, just as Anne had taken to dismissing her maid as soon as her corset was unlaced. Undressing each other had become a kind of game— which item went first, whose clothing came off faster, which items could be left on if the mood was one of swift attainment rather than leisurely exploration.

But Anne was in no mood for games tonight.

She pulled the door shut behind her, untied the belt of her robe and shrugged it from her shoulders. She was wearing nothing underneath.

Simon stopped dead, his eyes going dark and his fingers clenching the white linen at his neck like a flag of surrender.

"By the time I reach the bed," Anne said, "I expect you to be on it."

He gasped and stared, but by her second step he'd whipped his shirt off and hurled it to the floor. By her third step he'd lunged between the bedposts, using his weight to give him momentum. On her fourth step, Anne was within arm's length of the mattress and her husband was sprawled out on the coverlet, panting, his eyes wide and his chest heaving. At his wife's command, he yanked the buttons of his trousers open and sent the rest of his clothing tumbling to the floor.

She eyed his cock, starting to swell to attention between his spread thighs. "Hands over your head," she told him.

His voice was rough but he obeyed. "Yes, Countess." Simon turned so his head rested on the pillows and reached up, gripping the edge of the headboard. The strain brought out the muscles in the backs of his arms and brought tension to the curve of his stomach—Anne passed an approving hand across this span of warm flesh and smiled to see him quiver. She'd grown to crave the way he so cheerfully submitted to her, calling her *countess* all the while. It made her feel more at ease with the title, as though it were slowly becoming hers by right rather than by marriage. Firmly but not forcefully, she pushed Simon's knees apart and stepped between them. One hand gripped his cock, rolling her thumb over the head of it. "Don't move," she said.

Before he could reply, she bent down and took him in her mouth.

Simon gasped but held as still as he could. Small tremors rocked him as she sucked, relishing the salt flavor of his skin, his breath echoing the rhythmic movements of her tongue and lips. Her hand gripped his shaft, sliding up and down the length her mouth couldn't contain. With a moan he tried to buck up from the bed, pushing deeper into her mouth, but Anne put her free hand on his hip, holding him firmly in place and pricking him slightly with her nails as a reproof for this mild act of disobedience.

It did not take long before he was as hard as she wanted. Anne raised her head and moved forward onto the bed, straddling him, one hand still gripping his cock at the base. She got into position, steadied herself, took a deep breath and plunged down onto his cock in one swift, decisive motion.

Simon groaned. Anne bowed forward and hissed in pain. Her cunt wasn't ready, wasn't wet enough, and the usually pleasurable stretching was suddenly rough and strained.

Fingers tangled in her hair, tucking it behind her ears. "Countess," he murmured, rising on his elbows. Concern threaded his voice. "You don't have to—"

She cut him off with another plunge. A strangled sound came from his throat. Anne grabbed his hands and pressed them behind him on the bed. The pose pushed her breasts hard against his chest. Her nipples tightened at the contact but it wasn't enough to ease the pain between her legs. She gritted her teeth. "Don't move," she said again.

Again she lifted her body, dropped down, and again the pain slashed through her. And again. And again. Her shoulders shook and her hands clenched, tight on her husband's wrists, but she kept going. This pain was a sacrifice, she told herself. This pain was an offering, a test of her strength. She would not be defeated.

As she bit her lips and lifted the next time, Simon's cock slipped free of her body.

She stopped and peered down between their bodies. His cock had softened, not entirely but enough, and lay quiescent against his thigh. Anne lifted her eyes and met Simon's quiet gaze. He'd obeyed her and he hadn't moved, but it was abundantly clear that she'd managed to kill whatever pleasure he was feeling in the act.

The pain couldn't stop her but this could.

Anne buried her face in his shoulder, racked with sobs.

Simon said nothing at first, merely wrapped his arms tightly around her and held on, calm and peaceful as the night itself— while the storm of anguish inside Anne threatened to drag her down into a far more terrifying blackness. Her hands convulsively gripped and released him, her knees clenched around his waist, and never had she been more grateful for the whole sturdy bulk of his frame. Eventually she recovered enough of herself to feel embarrassed, and tried to scrub the tears and all the rest of it from her eyes and nose. "I'm so sorry," she said.

His eyes met hers, and there was worry in them but not an ounce of judgment. "Why didn't you want to stop?" he asked. "I could tell you were hurting."

Anne's gaze slid to his collarbone. "Just because something hurts doesn't mean it's wrong," she said.

His lips thinned. "But it doesn't mean it's right, either. Pain exists to tell us something." Large, warm hands moved up and down her arms, coming to rest on her shoulders. "What were you trying to tell me?"

Anne turned her head away and pushed herself off the bed,

reaching for her discarded clothing. Her robe was cool against the skin, so she moved to stand in front of the fire, at a safe distance from Simon. Her hands couldn't seem to stop twisting around each other, so she tucked them underneath her crossed arms. She intended to say something unobjectionable and placating, but it wasn't her nature. "Aren't you at all worried that we haven't conceived yet?" she burst out.

Behind her, the bed creaked, and before long she felt his hands on her shoulders, his chin on her head. "I've thought about it," he admitted, "but I wouldn't describe it as a worry."

She turned slightly to look up at him and allowed herself the luxury of leaning in to the warmth of his chest. "You need an heir, Simon."

"I have an heir. John will inherit should anything happen to me. And he has a child on the way, so there's a spare as well." Anne cringed a little, remembering Hecuba and Fiona and Nicholas. Simon squeezed her in reassurance. "And then there's Imogen," he went on, his tone light. "If something happens to John and his line, there's hope for the title in Imogen's offspring. Should she ever decide to stop traveling and produce offspring, of course."

"I had forgotten Imogen," Anne murmured.

Simon peered more closely at her. "This isn't really about the earldom, is it? Are you still worried about being the ideal countess?"

"The ideal countess would have given you triplets by now." Simon chuckled, but Anne's humor quickly evaporated. "But no, this isn't about the title or the estate or the succession. This is about me and what I want. I've wanted a family my whole life."

Her husband's hands were a warm weight on her shoulders. "You'll have one," Simon said, his voice low and steely. "That's a promise."

CHAPTER 11

Two days later, Hecuba's specialist arrived. He was a surprisingly short and broad-shouldered Scotsman by the name of Duncan Ver. A thin, long-faced woman he addressed only as Moira silently shadowed his every move. With a smile and a few remarks in a friendly burr, Dr. Ver marched into Hecuba's bedroom, shut the door in John's face, and spent several hours examining the expectant mother and asking a series of thorough questions.

At the doctor's request, Anne had a maid ready a basin of hot water with soap and a towel, and brought these things in herself when the door finally opened again. John rushed over to his wife, who grimaced as Dr. Ver nodded approval and began to wash his hands. "I can certainly see why Dr. Acton was concerned," he said, referring to the country physician who had recommended him to Hecuba, "but his experience is nowhere near the equal of mine in these matters. We'll keep an eye on things, but there is every reason to hope that both mother and babe will be just right in the end."

Anne was relieved to hear it—but she had an ulterior motive of her own. "Since you are so experienced in such things…" she began, keeping her voice low so as not to carry to the other side of the room.

Dr. Ver cocked one knowing, wiry eyebrow. "Are you expecting, my lady?"

Anne flushed and smoothed her skirts into place. "I wish I were. We…my husband and I…have been trying very hard."

"Ah." The doctor dried his hands and handed basin and towel to Moira, who began washing the various pieces of the doctor's medical kit. Various metal implements in strange and stomach-turning shapes gleamed and glinted beneath her hands. Anne pulled her eyes away with difficulty. "If you would permit me the liberty of a moment in private…" said Dr. Ver.

With a guilty glance at Hecuba and John, Anne showed the doctor and his shadow to her bedroom.

The examination was awkward, thorough, and thoroughly humiliating. Anne focused on taking deep breaths and trying not to worry that all her nether regions—guts, cunt and all her other amorphous organs—felt as though they were being squeezed in a vise, pulse-like, pressing and releasing by turns like the heartbeat of some demonic machine. Dr. Ver muttered occasional asides to Moira, who would hand him one instrument or another, but mostly from what little Anne let herself deduce without actually looking he seemed to be using his hands, prodding and stretching and poking at the tenderest parts of her. He was quite adept at finding the sorest spots and lingering there, especially just above her hips on either side. It was excruciating but Anne refused to let any sound pain emerge from her clenched teeth. Tears prickled in the corners of her eyes—she attempted to surreptitiously wipe them away, but looked up with clearer sight to catch the doctor's glance of sympathy.

"Yes, it can't be comfortable for you, I know," he said. This acknowledgement somehow allowed her to forgive him most of the discomfort. Anne sat up and put herself to rights, opened the door for another maid with a fresh basin, and took a seat in a chair to await the doctor's verdict. Moira and Dr. Ver repeated their hygienic ballet while the countess fidgeted silently. At length the Scotsman turned back to her and took the seat next to hers, calm radiating off him like mist from a mountain. "How are your courses, my lady?"

"I beg your pardon?" The shock was instant, but she squelched it down. Of course he was going to ask intrusive questions—that was his duty as a physician. There was no sense in punishing him for it.

Mercifully, he appeared not to mark her rudeness. "How frequently do you have them?"

Anne steeled herself against embarrassment. "Once every two months, more or less. Sometimes they are farther apart, but not usually."

He showed no reaction to this information but moved on to the next question. "Are they predictable or do they take you by surprise?"

"They are not nearly as predictable as I would like," Anne said tartly. Moira smothered a smile. "But they are not so varied as to be entirely unexpected."

He nodded a little. "Are they very painful?"

Anne's lips thinned. "Quite."

He nodded again, more deeply. As though he had expected it. Unease bloomed low in Anne's belly. "My lady," he said, "you should prepare yourself for the probability that you may never have children."

Never have children. The echo of that pronouncement plugged her ears like cotton wool. She felt rather than heard herself reply. "Probability?" she said. "Not possibility?" A spark of angry denial burned the cotton clean away. "Not impossibility?"

The doctor nodded again. "Over the years, I have seen a few cases similar to yours. It happens when..." He tilted his head. "How specific would you like me to be?"

"As precise as you can." Anne fought to breathe normally. Her heart was already racing in her chest and the cotton wool was growing back.

Dr. Ver considered for a moment. "Your symptoms match those of a number of women I have seen," he said. "Painful courses, not always on schedule, and a great deal of tenderness in certain parts of your abdomen. These areas here," he said, and sketched two short diagonal lines above the bones of each of her hips. "Nobody knows the cause—many of my colleagues are even skeptical that this condition exists, and those who acknowledge it argue constantly about what form it commonly takes—but from what I have personally noticed, the women who share your symptoms are almost never blessed with children." A brief moment of pity colored his eyes.

Anne wanted to shout that she didn't care about pain or probability, so long as there was a child. The air in the room was getting thinner and thinner, her heart going faster and faster, careening down this dark path toward the jagged cliffs over the sea. "Is there a cure?"

Dr. Ver snorted, his Scottish stoicism more palpable than ever. "A cure for something many refuse to believe is even a real disease?" He shook his head. "My profession bristles with conflicting opinions, and I am considered a dangerous radical in most circles. I wish I could offer you hope, my lady, any hope at all—but I dare not."

Moira had finished repacking the instruments into their carrying case, so Dr. Ver now rose from his seat, bowed low and took his leave.

Anne was left battered, breathless and alone.

Never have children. The words buzzed around her, swirling hot and angry in the air. If she didn't leave the room, if she didn't get up from her seat, if she didn't so much as breathe, perhaps they would get bored and fly away elsewhere. Perhaps her life would be what it was meant to be" surrounded by little ones, in a house full of noise and toys and trouble and laughter. If Anne could have taken a blade and opened her veins to undo this curse, she wouldn't have hesitated.

But the blood she was so eager to spill came from a body that had betrayed her. Her most deeply cherished dream, toward which she'd strived and worked ever since she was old enough to know her own mind, had crumbled into dust before she could grasp it.

The pit yawned beneath her, black and bottomless. If she let herself get too near the edge, she would fall in and be lost forever.

Anne pushed herself up from the chair. *Never have children—* she shoved the echoes away and put on her countess face. One step toward the door, then another, then another. A hand on the knob. A twist and a pull to open. Simple gestures, confidently made. One step at a time down the hallway, toward the room where Hecuba and John were waiting. There was a meal to see to, a tray to provide for Hecuba, and several dinner courses to arrange for herself, her husband, and her brother-in-law. John and Simon would take brandy and cigars afterward. Anne would head upstairs and sit with Hecuba. Easy, familiar tasks, so deeply ingrained as to be rote, that required no thought or planning or feeling to accomplish.

She must set her feet carefully on this high and stony road, never once looking back at the pit behind her. To look back was to be swallowed whole.

To look back was to lose everything.

By the following morning, Anne could feel the mask beginning to crack. Fiona wasn't scheduled to come by until tomorrow and Hecuba was barricaded in her room again. Simon and John had gone riding—one of them had bought a new horse, she hadn't marked who—and they would not be back for some time. Anne was left unbearably empty-handed. She had to do something, to be somewhere, anywhere else. She didn't dare to stop moving.

So she put on her green striped day silk with the ruched black belt, ordered the carriage and went to visit Mrs. Bell, who hadn't yet left town.

The nearly spherical butler—what was his name? Anne couldn't recall—took her card and bowed. Anne thought he looked like a globe slowly turning on its equator. It was strangely hypnotic. "I shall see if madam is at home," he said. Anne was left stewing in the foyer, toying with the end of her shawl, tugging at the hem of one glove with the other.

And then she heard it—a giggle, and not a quiet one, from the direction of the front parlor.

There was something about that giggle she most assuredly did not trust.

The butler returned, politely accepting her gloves and shawl. "If you'll follow me please, Lady Underwood," he said. He led Anne to the same parlor where the giggle had come from, an airy little room all windows and wainscoting, decorated in white and robin's-egg blue. Mrs. Bell was there, wearing dark blue wool, and on the couch beside her...

It was Lady Audley, glowing in yellow taffeta with ivory trim. Her eyes were as bright as knives and her smile showed none of her teeth.

"The Countess of Underwood," announced the butler.

Anne hesitated. Besides Mrs. Bell and Lady Audley there were two other ladies, in orange-flowered cotton and delicate pink brocade. One of them was leaning forward eagerly and the other was blushing, her eyes cast down to one side. The energy in the air was palpable and, to Anne, entirely puzzling.

Mrs. Bell rose from the sofa and offered her hands, which Anne clasped gratefully. "I hope I am not intruding," she said. It was one of the useful phrases she'd learned from Fiona. "I have been keeping too much to myself of late and felt in need of society."

"Of course, my dear," said Mrs. Bell, and drew Anne to a seat in an empty chair. "I don't believe you've met Miss Georgiana Gilroy or her sister, Miss Louisa."

"How do you do?" murmured Miss Gilroy, the one in orange. Her pink sister merely blushed harder and nodded.

Anne murmured a polite response, but her attention was still on Lady Audley's smile. "Lady Underwood," the woman purred. "We were just talking about that handsome husband of yours."

This, at least, was not puzzling. That was satisfaction, rich and buttery and malicious, oozing out from between Lady Audley's rosy lips. "Were you?" Anne replied, aiming for nonchalance but not quite striking the target. "Simon will be pleased that you remember him so fondly."

"It's hard to forget a man like his lordship," Lady Audley continued, while Mrs. Bell began to pour a cup of tea for Anne.

"Or his lordship's brother," Miss Gilroy piped up, her eagerness getting the better of her.

Anne froze, one hand in midair reaching for the teacup. Mrs. Bell pressed it on her, frowning gently at Lady Audley before she caught herself and smoothed the expression. "Yes, we all remember Mr. Rushmore quite fondly from prior years," she said.

Miss Louisa finally lifted her eyes to meet Anne's. They were fine eyes, gray and lustrous. All at once the girl was pretty beyond all reason. "He danced with me once, at my first ball," she said. "I was terrified of stepping on his toes, but he told me that gentlemen considered bruises of the feet to be wounds earned in honorable service." The eyes fell and the glamor was banished.

"Yes," Anne said, her hands curling around the comforting warmth of the teacup. "That sounds like John."

"Always so charming," Lady Audley interjected. "It was such a shame that he behaved so abominably to your cousin." Her smile grew a little before she elegantly reined it in. "And such a shame that he is now merely a tradesman. Turning his back on his noble birth—it must have been quite appalling for all of you."

"Mmm." Anne sipped her tea, letting the warmth of it fill the hollow ache inside her.

Lady Audley was not so easily put off. "With such a stain on his character, I wonder that your husband sees fit to associate with him again."

"We saw them," Miss Gilroy confessed, excitement thrumming

through her. "Riding near Hyde Park. It was definitely Mr. Rushmore."

"I expected better of the earl, really I did," said Lady Audley smoothly. She tilted her head confidentially. "No wonder you haven't been about much lately," she said to Anne. "I wouldn't care to be seen in such distasteful company either." With this parting shot, she leaned back comfortably in her chair, hiding her smile beneath an elegant tilt of her teacup.

"It can happen in the best of families," Mrs. Bell said soothingly.

"But what kind of example does it set for the younger ones?" Lady Audley asked. "Miss Louisa, for instance, is so delicate and impressionable."

"You are, Louisa," Miss Gilroy chimed in. She had also leaned back in her chair and taken a sip from her tea, her eyes still on Lady Audley.

The lady went on. "What sort of behavior should we teach her to expect from the gentlemen of her class? No, there must be standards, and we are all responsible for maintaining them."

Mrs. Bell smiled. "It's certainly far too important a job to leave up to the men. They haven't the sensitivity or subtlety for it." Lady Audley laughed appreciatively. Mrs. Bell turned her smile on Anne. "But they can be reasoned with when they are in the mood. The earl is clearly devoted to you, my dear. I'm certain he'll consider your point of view most carefully." Mrs. Bell then tactfully changed the subject, quizzing both Miss Gilroy and her sister about which young men were their current favorites among the crop of young and eligible suitors.

Anne drained the last of her tea but kept the cup in her hands. Porcelain was beautiful, but so fragile. It chipped or cracked at the least little injury, and once broken it could rarely be made good as new. Apparently reputations were made of similar stuff.

Mrs. Bell was at present warning Miss Louisa that her tendency to wander out onto the balconies of ballrooms could lead to damaging rumors and innuendo. "I like the stars," Miss

Louisa replied. "And that's the only way I can see them when we're in London."

"Yes, dear, but it leaves you out of sight of your chaperone," Mrs. Bell replied. "And to be always hanging about on the edges of things can give certain gentlemen...unpleasant ideas."

"You wouldn't want to spoil your chances at a good match, would you?" Lady Audley said. "Or your sister's?" Miss Gilroy looked alarmed and began to prod for more details, which Louisa did not seem eager to supply.

All at once Anne ran out of patience. "Do you have a favorite star?" she interrupted.

Three pairs of indignant eyes turned toward her.

Miss Louisa's eyes warmed, however. "Perhaps it's a bit obvious, but I like the pole star," she said. "It's the easiest to find. And it tells me which way north is, which is so useful."

"When could that possibly be useful?" Miss Gilroy demanded.

"On a ship," her sister replied, her gaze going unfocused and dreamy.

"I mean useful to you," Miss Gilroy muttered.

Louisa was too far away to hear. "In the middle of the ocean, or a tropical jungle—"

"Or the Arctic," Anne added.

Louisa grinned and nodded. "I should love to see the Arctic," she said. "Perhaps I might discover the Northwest Passage."

"That would be very useful," Anne agreed.

"But not, I think, a proper occupation for a young lady of quality." Mrs. Bell's voice was kind enough, but the light went out of Louisa's eyes again.

Anne left soon after that. She'd hoped for a day of comfort and distraction but she returned home feeling even more troubled than when she'd left. She knew that thanks to Lady Audley, the story of John and Simon's reconciliation would be played as a tragedy, not as a redemption tale. This was not the prodigal son returning for absolution but the corruption spreading to blight the entire family tree.

The family's future would be blighted with it.

But now a rebellious thought was pushing its way up to the surface: what future, precisely?

If she couldn't have children, whose future was she risking by welcoming John and Hecuba back into the family bosom? Only hers and Simon's—but Simon didn't seem particularly to care about society, especially not now that he and John were on good terms again. Anne had cared for society's approval, but today had made clear to her the sheer amount of effort involved in keeping one's good name polished and ready for display. It was a daily battle in a war that never ended.

She was too exhausted to help to uphold Lady Audley's high standards, it seemed. Let them be guarded by women like Miss Gilroy, who had energy, and Mrs. Bell, who had the skill. All Anne had was enough strength to put one foot in front of the other, to keep herself just barely on the path.

What a lackluster countess she'd become.

CHAPTER 12

*D*r. Ver and the silent Moira came by the house every day, though these subsequent visits were much briefer than the first. On the afternoon after the fourth such visit, Hecuba's labor began.

The doctor and his assistant were called and dispatched upstairs. Anne went along to help to coordinate the servants' efforts and provide support and encouragement to Hecuba. Dr. Ver had expressly forbidden John from attending the birth —"Once had an anxious husband punch me right in the mouth, since the worry-crazed fool thought I was torturing his wife," he explained—so it became Simon's job to keep his brother distracted as best he could.

They were waiting in the study, looking at the new paintings John had brought along as a belated wedding present. Simon was trying to decide which ones Nicholas would like best, a process made infinitely more difficult by the artist himself, who was pacing back and forth across the room, his country boots making entirely more noise than necessary. "Sit down and have a brandy, John," said the earl.

"While my wife is upstairs, in agony, risking her life and the life of my child?" His brother shook his head. "Simon, if I have one brandy, I'm going to want *all* the brandy."

"Have all the brandy then. You might as well—it'll be hours yet."

"How do you know?" John snapped, but at least he stopped pacing. He spun around instead to glare at his brother. "How many births have you attended?"

Simon lifted both hands in a gesture of surrender. "You've caught me. Half the urchin population of London are my by-blows. I'm only waiting until they get a little older, then I'll turn them into an army to take vengeance upon wealthy aristocrats who think themselves above the law."

John snorted and resumed his pacing. "You sound like one of Hecuba's Gothic novels."

"So do you," Simon returned. "Your wife is going to be just fine."

"You can't know that," John protested.

"Of course I do. Can you imagine how furious she'd be if she died?" Simon demanded. "Death might turn up, but she'd start yelling as soon as she realized who he was, and he'd drop the scythe to clap both hands over his ears, and Hecuba would lurch out of bed and chase Death away, then use the scythe to cut the cord." The small smile that appeared on his brother's wan face made Simon want to shout with triumph. He hurried to keep that relaxation in place. "Besides, if you ask me, you should be much more worried about what happens *after* your child arrives."

Simon had deliberately given his pronouncement the dark weight of earned and terrible knowledge. John blinked in response. "How do you mean?"

"A baby warps all the world around it," Simon said. "It's a tiny little demon with an insatiable appetite. The mouth is almost never closed—either it's producing vast, ear-bursting amounts of noise, or it's drooling, or it's wrapped around something valuable or breakable or poisonous. And if nothing's coming out of one end, chances are it's coming out of the other. Have you ever once in your life changed a nappy?" he asked. "You will. Quite frequently. You will discover colors of excrement you never knew existed—a whole new spectrum of disgust, past even your talents as a painter to capture." John snorted again. Simon warmed to his theme. "And this is only the beginning, only the stuff I've witnessed firsthand. Mrs. Walker tells me Nicholas is starting to learn to push himself up from the floor on his hands and knees. Soon enough he'll be crawling, then walking. Do you know how many corners there are in your house? How many trailing ends of tablecloths or sharp implements lying within reach of greedy little hands? It's a wonder any of us survive past the age of four." John's brow was starting to furrow again with concern, so Simon changed tacks. "And then there's the question of how long until Hecuba recovers enough for you to resume your husbandly duties…"

John grinned. "No need to be worried there," he said. "Hecuba can be very creative about such things."

There was a pause as both men considered the conversational road that had opened up in front of them.

"Shall we change the subject?" John asked.

"Do let's," Simon replied at once. He turned back to the new paintings and heaved one up onto the desk. "This latest painting has to be your most atrocious yet."

"You have the worst taste for art I've ever seen," John countered with gusto. "Do you know, I am thinking of showing you all my paintings and pricing them accordingly? The ones you hate are by far my most acclaimed and popular pieces."

They bickered happily for the rest of the evening, taking a quiet meal right where they were. Anne remained upstairs, though Simon inquired of the servants and made sure that she had taken the time to eat something. John was eventually persuaded to have a brandy, and then another, and then another as time passed and the wee hours of the night came and went. He fell asleep in front of the study's crackling fire, head nodding forward, dark circles beneath his eyes. Simon tucked a blanket around him, instructed a footman to wait outside the door in case he needed anything, and took himself to bed.

But he couldn't sleep.

Just down the hall, his sister-in-law was bringing a new life into this world. He'd grown so accustomed to the miracle of Nicholas that he'd lost sight of what a marvel it was that women could actually produce other human beings, knitted together from their own flesh, bone and blood. No wonder there were so many things written in praise of mothers—the act of creation was a sobering, awe-inspiring power.

Nor was it without risks. For all his earlier flippancy, Simon knew that bearing children was the most dangerous undertaking in many women's lives. Even when it wasn't fatal, it was uncomfortable at best and agonizingly painful at worst. John was right to be worried about his wife.

Simon was suddenly overwhelmed by a wave of humility that his countess was willing to do something so frightening on his behalf. He ached with the yearning to offer her something in return for such a gift. When the day came, he'd be as terrified as his brother was now—but until that moment, he could at least focus on making the rest of the experience as wonderful as possible.

Including—perhaps especially—the conception.

Simon still hurt to think of their last encounter. While he was grateful for the revelations that had followed their abortive attempt at lovemaking, he knew the whole episode had been frustrating for Anne, even more than for him. He'd grown up with the title and all its expectations, but she was still fairly new to the pressure and the sense of having to live up to an impossible standard. He didn't need her to be the ideal countess she was struggling to become—but he did need her to be comfortable in the role, however she came to define it.

So. Just telling her not to worry had not soothed her, or at least not enough. But Simon knew, deep in his bones, that if Anne conceived she would feel relieved of a large part of her anxiety.

He couldn't make that happen, at least not by sheer force of will, but he had to do something.

John would know precisely how to go about it, he thought. John had been an accomplished rake in his younger days, popular with widows and courtesans and some of the bolder, unhappily married ladies of the *ton*.

There was no way in hell he was going to ask his brother for advice on pleasuring his countess.

But John had also been an artist, and one prone to more erotic subjects than were strictly proper for a gentleman of his birth and bloodline. Simon knew a few volumes of illicit lithographs, sketches and stories still lurked in his library, cunningly hidden amid the sermons and the Shakespeare and the vast desert of pedantic prose his ancestors had carefully collected and bound in calf and gilt.

While Anne was occupied with her cousin, there was time for Simon to do research.

As always, having made a decision and a plan settled his anxious thoughts. The earl tucked himself beneath the covers and closed his eyes.

At a little past five in the morning, Hecuba was delivered of a beautiful baby girl, with a light dusting of noticeably red hair. "That might change," Dr. Ver warned as Moira set the wailing infant in its exhausted mother's arms.

"I hope not," Hecuba retorted, sounding almost as impertinent as usual, and she and the Scotsman shared a conspiratorial grin.

Anne felt as though the long night hours had picked her up and squeezed all the life out of her. She watched her cousin coo nonsensical things to the tiny infant she held, brushing wondering fingers over ears, nose, cheeks and bunching baby fists. "Do you know what you're going to name her?" Anne asked.

Hecuba nodded, though her eyes stayed on the child. "We

were thinking Phoebe for a first name," she said, then glanced up, face lit with a hopeful glow. "And Anne for a middle name. If you wouldn't mind." She adjusted little Phoebe Anne's position slightly. Her face was still flushed from the effort of giving birth, her red hair was straggly and bronze, yet the glow of happiness on her face made her luminously, profoundly beautiful, like a Madonna in a Renaissance masterpiece.

Up until that moment, Anne had forgotten about the pit. An ominous wind seemed to brush skeletal fingers against the back of her neck, chilling her despite the sweltering heat of the room. *Never have children.* "I would be honored," she managed to say through the ashes that filled her mouth. Hecuba smiled her thanks, her attention already more than half returned to the baby.

It was suddenly too much. Anne struggled to her feet as Dr. Ver slanted a gaze her way. "Thank you for all your help, Lady Underwood," he said. "Please don't let us keep you from seeking your own bed. You've had a very long night."

The undercurrent of sympathy rankled, though she knew the doctor meant well. *One step at a time*, Anne thought. "I think I'll go down to the kitchens for breakfast and tea instead," she said calmly. "I'll have them send up a tray for you and Moira as well."

Dr. Ver nodded but his attention was already back on the new mother and new child. As Anne shut the door behind her, she could hear the beginning of a long list of instructions Hecuba was to follow for her recuperation. Anne could only hope someone more steady than she presently was would think to write these things down.

She sent a footman in search of the happy father and descended to the kitchens.

Breakfast helped but not enough. Something hard and round had lodged in her chest beneath her breastbone, making it impossible to breathe properly. For a moment she teetered on the edge of the cliff.

One step at a time.

She pushed the last half-piece of toast aside and thanked Cook.

The next two weeks were a blur of exhaustion, but finally Hecuba was well enough and the babe strong enough to travel home, where the wet nurse and respite awaited them. Hecuba was already anxious to return to her chemical formulae, and John could hardly wait to get his hands on his paints again now that he had an engrossing subject.

He'd already littered Simon's study with sketches of his new daughter—Phoebe sleeping, Phoebe crying, Phoebe cuddling with her mother.

Phoebe in the arms of her upright aunt, whose faint frown made her as stern as a Gothic governess.

John had laughed at the contrast, but Anne was perfectly torn between relief and despair. It had been torturous to watch from the outside as Hecuba and John reveled in the new shape of their family. If her cousin had been staying longer, Anne might have found the courage to unburden herself about Dr. Ver's diagnosis. But that dark anguish was of the pit and it had no right to cloud this joyous first morning of young Phoebe's life. So Anne had bitten her lip, reminded herself she was a countess and ignored everything but the task at hand: keeping five distracted people cleaned, clothed and fed.

Her reward? A house vacant of everything but echoes, with summer fading into fall.

And now the carriage was being brought around. John was on the step, manfully directing the arranging of boxes and luggage and the large hamper Cook had put together for the journey. Hecuba was bouncing slightly in place, while Phoebe napped on her shoulder. She held out one hand to Anne and squeezed, her eyes filling.

Anne squeezed back, her heart cracking slightly. She had only just gotten her cousin back—must she really lose her again so soon? And for what—the conditional approval of people like Lady Audley? Such a tawdry reward. Anne made up her mind and cast respectability to the winds. "You will join us for Christmas at Marlston, won't you?" she asked her cousin.

Hecuba sobered. "Are you sure?" She waved a hand at the marble foyer and the bustling pack of servants. "You've come so far up in the world—a countess, a London hostess, eminently respectable. I know how much you've fought for this security, how much you've wanted it." Her green eyes met Anne's with just a hint of challenge. "Are you really prepared to risk it all just for one Christmas?"

Anne's mouth thinned. "Not for one Christmas, no. For every Christmas. For every one of Phoebe's birthdays. For your next child's birthdays too." She wrapped both her hands around Hecuba's one, words pouring out of her now. "I've tried respectability and found it wanting, my dear cousin, because you are not there to share it with me. I miss you and I refuse to go on making both of us miserable just to satisfy people who have no true place in our hearts. I'm sorry I ever let anything so trivial as a scandal come between us. For Phoebe's sake, can you forgive me?"

Hecuba laughed and kissed the back of Anne's hand. "There's nothing to forgive," she said. "I've missed you too." She grinned, her old boldness coming to the fore. "If you ever want to really shock your society friends, I am always available for dinners and parties."

"I will accept that challenge," Anne replied, and hugged her cousin farewell.

It was on the seventh night that Simon truly began to worry.

Anne had not seemed quite her usual self, but he'd attributed that to exhaustion from the trying times of Hecuba's lying-in. And he had his library research to occupy him—titillating though it was, he had yet to find something that felt more daring or different from many of the things they'd already tried with each other. But on the fifth evening after Hecuba's departure, when Anne lay down silently beside him in the bed, his need got the better of him and he curled himself behind her, nuzzling her neck and sliding his hands from his waist to her breasts.

With a murmur, she turned toward him. But what started as a gentle, lazy game of seduction ended with Anne sitting on the edge of the bed, weeping, her arms wrapped around her knees, refusing to talk about what was wrong.

Simon ached inside but didn't press her. The next night she attempted to seduce him, pushing him down into a chair by the fire and straddling his eager hips.

Again it ended with Anne wiping away tears and Simon horribly adrift with confusion.

He couldn't figure out what had happened, but after three days he didn't particularly care how or why. He just wanted it to stop.

He wanted his countess back.

And there was only one person who could find her.

So the next morning, when she was only just awake, he drew the curtains to let the morning light into the room and said, "Please, Anne, tell me what's wrong."

She made some sleepy reply but it wasn't English, just some collection of vowels and consonants he couldn't decipher.

His seated weight bowed down the bed and made her roll toward him. She rubbed her knuckle against her eyes, scowling. Simon wanted to pull her into his arms, but he wasn't certain he should just yet. "Has something happened?" he asked. "Is it something I've done?"

"What? No," she mumbled, leaning up on one elbow, blankets and linens bunched up around her and wrinkled from the weight of the night.

Simon went on relentlessly. "Is it something someone else has done? Hecuba or John?" A horrifying possibility asserted itself in his brain, making him catch his breath.

Anne's eyes widened as she caught his expression. "No, Simon

—nobody's done anything. Nobody *can* do anything," she went on, then flushed and turned away as if she hadn't meant those words to come out.

Simon's large hand covered hers and he nearly expired of relief to feel her fingers tighten around his. But he knew they were still in the woods. "Nobody can do anything about what?" he asked.

Anne's voice was low and flat, carefully scrubbed of all emotion. "On Dr. Ver's first visit I asked him to examine me too," she said. "I was worried because we've been married so long and we've been so…active, yet still my womb has yet to quicken. And he said…" Simon could sense the end of this confession, a dark place at the end of a long tunnel, but he waited to hear her say the words. "He thinks I won't ever have children." Anne let out a breath on a long, shuddering sigh. "Simon, he believes I'm barren."

And there it was. There was a world before and a world after her confession, and they were no longer the same. It took him a moment to find his bearings in this new geography. He'd always wanted children—but in a distant way, the same way he'd wanted a well-sprung carriage and an elegant house and a proper, presentable wife. All those things seemed appropriate to the earldom, the necessary trappings for a title and a peer. It was how one was recognized by the world, the same way that a bust of Hadrian could be recognized by the beard.

But…did he really want children for himself?

He'd wanted them with Anne, Simon realized, because he'd wanted them *for* Anne, because she wanted them with every fiber of her being. And if he was stunned and shocked by the news, her own sense of loss must be nearly overpowering. And she'd known for weeks, since Hecuba's arrival and through the birth and everything that followed after. A spur of anger that she hadn't trusted him, hadn't depended on him to help her burned through him, but vanished again as quickly as a comet passing across the dark night sky.

She was looking at him with reddened eyes brimful of tears she hadn't shed yet. "Well?" she asked.

He knew the sound of someone spoiling for a fight. He also knew a fight was preferable to this quiet despair she'd wrapped herself in. "Well what?" he responded.

"Simon, I can't give you an heir." Her chin had lifted, just a little.

Simon shrugged as casually as he knew how. "I've told you before—I have an heir." For extra provocation, he pulled his hand from hers and stretched out on his back in the bed, folding his arms above his head in a position of false nonchalance.

It worked. Her brow turned thunderous. He could all but feel the rage starting to simmer in her veins. "I don't think you're taking this seriously," she said.

"Do I need to? It seems you're taking this seriously enough for both of us."

Her fists clenched in the bedclothes. Almost there... "You should find yourself another countess," she blurted.

Now it was out, thankfully. Simon wondered how long she had been carrying that thought around like a viper in her breast. "That is an impossibility," he replied. He'd cut out his own heart before he'd willingly give her up.

"We can get an annulment," she went on, interpreting his resistance as merely a lack of solutions to the puzzle. "We could tell them I'm refusing you your husbandly rights."

"Do you really think there are no witnesses the court might call to refute that?" Simon asked with a snort. "Servants, friends... Annulments are fiendishly difficult. And no," he said, holding up a hand to stall her next inevitable suggestion, "I'm not rich or important enough to divorce you by an Act of Parliament either." He rolled to his side, facing her, eyes meeting hers. "I love you, Anne Rushmore. You are my countess and you always will be."

Anne didn't sigh or blush or wilt with relief, as he'd half-hoped, but stayed statue-still in bed. Her eyes were distant, her tone even and cold. "You don't understand," she said. "I can't *be* your countess anymore. I can hardly be myself anymore." Her shoulders were stiff, her hands still fisted in the sheets. "Ever since I learned, whenever you've touched me, I haven't been able to...I can't react or enjoy it, even though I try to. I can't forget that the body you're touching isn't capable of doing the most important thing I wanted it to do. My body has betrayed me and I don't know how to forgive it." Her lips pressed together for a moment. "I'm sorry I cannot give you a family, Simon."

Simon's false belligerence drained away. He could live without children—he couldn't live without Anne. He sat up and grabbed her hands again. "You are my family."

She smiled at his reassurance but her eyes slid sideways and he knew she only smiled to humor him.

The rest of that day was a blur of preparation for the trip into the country. Simon hadn't personally visited his property at Marlston for some time, and Anne had never seen the other homes she had acquired along with her husband's name. Packing was never easy for an earl and his countess, but today Simon's brains were occupied less with quantities of coats or shirts or stockings and more by the weightier problem of how to reconcile with his despairing and distant wife. And then, while scouring the library for more erotic volumes to pack—he was not at all certain the library at Marlston was similarly equipped—he dropped one. It tumbled to the ground, spine-up, pages bent at awkward angles like broken limbs. Simon winced and retrieved the book, then stopped as something about one of the sketches caught his eye.

He turned the book right side up and smoothed out the page for a better look. And choked. And stared. And took a deep breath. And stared some more, as fear and curiosity and a damn insistent arousal warred for his attention.

A knock at the door startled him out of his reverie, and as he looked at the fall of light on the study carpet he realized some time had passed. The knock was Phillips, inquiring as to whether his lordship needed more crates for books or whether the one he had would be enough. Simon slipped the book surreptitiously into his coat pocket. "Just the one crate will be fine, thank you," he told the butler, then paused. "Phillips?"

The butler cocked an eyebrow at the perfect angle to convey mild, incurious attentiveness. "Yes, my lord?"

Damn, but this was an awkward question. Simon steeled himself—nothing ventured, after all. "Phillips, you know that my brother used to have his valet Vickery procure certain...items...for his artwork? *Objets d'art*, sketchbooks, things of a more... adventurous nature than most art galleries or bookshops would carry?" By the color in Phillips' face, Simon had succeeded in making himself understood. He wondered if Phillips had ever seen some of his brother's more daring still lifes—but he couldn't get distracted now. The earl barreled ahead. "Do you happen to know where he went to find them?"

Phillips cleared his throat, smoothing every atom of expression from his face. "I believe there is a bookseller in the West End, on Cambridge Street, that sells items of that nature." The butler went even redder. "Does your lordship require me to—"

"No," Simon cut him off. "No, I will take care of this myself, thank you, Phillips." He could feel his own cheeks starting to turn red—an earl, blushing at his own butler! "If you could just provide me with the address..."

Phillips bowed silently and beat a retreat.

CHAPTER 13

*A*nne had never felt so faded by fatigue in all her life. Three days bouncing across the south of England in even the most well-sprung rig was not conducive to rest and recovery. She felt wraithlike, wrung out, a ghost in the house. Worse, rather than the crumbling walls and wind-swept grounds she'd expected, Marlston was a cozy little manor set in a beautifully wooded collection of hills. Any walk of five minutes' duration was sure to lead her across a sparkling brook or by a mirror-bright pond or through a grove of silver birches turned fiery bronze in honor of autumn. It was absurdly, infuriatingly picturesque, and Anne wished she had the energy to hate it.

But all she seemed capable of doing was sitting by the window, staring at the setting sun while an undrunk cup of tea went cool in her hands.

Today her husband had gone out early, riding the borders of the estate, visiting tenants and checking fences with his steward Mr. Holloway—who then joined them for dinner and stifled all but the most polite vein of conversation. Afterward the two men had retired to talk over some much-needed improvements. Anne had gone upstairs to wrap herself in her green woolen dressing gown and stare out of her bedroom window, which faced the darkened forest and was therefore even less interesting to the eye than sunset from the parlor.

Simon came in eventually and put a warm hand on her shoulder. "Do you like Marlston?" he asked.

What a question. She couldn't remember what it felt like to like or not like something. She was just so tired. "It's very wild," she replied.

"And old," he added. His tone was calm but there was something that buzzed beneath it and drew her attention. She craned her neck to peer up at him. Her husband was clearly suppressing a smile, trying and failing to look severe, with a quirk to the corners of his mouth and a twinkle in his eye. "I confess, the antiquity has certain advantages."

A tiny ember of curiosity awoke inside her. Just a single spark, but it was something other than darkness. "Such as?"

"Thick stone walls, heavily insulated—against the cold, but it has the convenient effect of muffling sound as well." His smile emerged from hiding. "One could scream for hours and nobody would hear a thing."

Anne sighed. She hated to disappoint him again, but she felt so far away from the world, so distant. It was wearing her down. "I don't feel much like screaming, Simon."

"I know," he said, and she relaxed a little at the understanding in his voice. But he only smiled wider. "I was thinking *I* might do the screaming."

She narrowed her eyes at him. What was he talking about?

He walked to the wardrobe and drew out a small wooden box. The top slid open silently, and from her place by the window Anne caught a glimpse of a plush cream velvet interior. Simon set the box on a long table at the foot of the overstuffed feather bed. Then he reached inside and drew something out. Anne's eyes at first refused to make sense of it—what on earth could...

It was a cock. Made of dark red wood, heavily varnished until it shone. It had a flared base decorated with small touches of gilt that gave it an impossibly hedonistic character, like something out of a pagan fairy tale, or a saint's nightmare. In length it was larger than a finger but smaller than Simon's cock, and not as thick around.

It was beautiful—she wouldn't have expected that, but it was. Graceful lines, smoothly rounded head, lustrously polished, a true artistic achievement. The candlelight made it flicker as though it were slightly alive. Simon set it quietly on the table beside its case. For the first time in weeks, Anne felt her pulse quicken with the well-known rhythm of desire. "And what do you suggest I do with that?" she asked.

Simon's grin flashed at the slight huskiness in her voice. "I suggest you use it on me."

Anne blinked. She couldn't have heard that correctly.

Simon reached into his coat pocket and pulled out a small volume, bound in very worn calf, which he held out to her. Anne took it and opened it to the page marked, which was a carefully done sketch of...

Anne pulled in a breath cold and sharp with shock. It was a man, nude but for a pair of sandals in the ancient style, bent over some invisible support. His broad thighs were spread wide, his arms pulled forward and bound in front of him. It was not an easy pose—the artist's hand had lovingly traced over every taut sinew and tense muscle and colored him with the sheen of sweat. But least comfortable of all, to Anne's eye, was the large cock thrust into the man's arse from behind. Someone else's hand—a man? another woman? impossible to tell—was splayed on his lower back, holding him in place for the invasion.

And this was what her husband wanted her to do to him? Anne looked more carefully and raised an eyebrow to see that not only was his face twisted with the erotic agony of near-climax, but his cock was erect and rampant in front of him.

She glanced up at Simon. He was watching her calmly, with only the slightest flavor of expectation in the way he held himself straight and tall. But she'd learned his body well in the past few months—the signs were clear. He wanted this. There was a telltale tension in his shoulders and an unembarrassed flush in his cheeks.

Before she could articulate her realization, he began to speak. "You said that your body had betrayed you," he rumbled in that low voice of his. "I don't know how to fix that. So I won't try. But I can do this—I can offer you my body instead. Until yours belongs to you again."

Anne looked back at the sketch. It was less startling now, and more intriguing. She remembered Simon's hand between her legs, and a few long-ago nights where his fingers had…strayed somewhat out of their usual course. The sensations had been different, but not unpleasant. Her heart gave a leap in her breast. She felt the blood rush through her, pumping in the pulse points at her wrists and throat and between her thighs.

She lifted her head again and eyed her husband's sturdy form. "You will begin by removing your clothes," she commanded.

"Yes, Countess." Relief and anticipation flashed in his eyes.

He stripped while she rose from her seat and moved the foot of the bed. She picked up the wooden cock and ran her fingers along the length, checking the finish, feeling for the least bit of roughness or friction. A splinter in this scenario would be a catastrophe.

"There's a small jar of oil in the box," her husband offered.

He was right, but she put on a stern expression anyway and put the dildo down. "From now on you will ask my permission before you say anything aside from, 'Yes, Countess.'"

Naked from the waist up now, he shivered a little. "Yes, Countess."

Anne smiled her approval.

She opened the jar as he removed his trousers, socks and smallclothes. The oil was sweetly scented and smooth to the touch. She set the jar aside for now and turned to the bed just as her husband stretched out, fully naked, hands at his side and his eyes fixed on her.

Oh, she had forgotten how it felt to be the focus of that

expectation. A banner of warmth unfurled within her and her feet were firm on the ground for the first time in what felt like decades. She lifted a hand and beckoned to him. He scooted to the edge of the bed and sat up, facing her. Anne untied her belt and turned her back to him. "Hold this," she said.

Obediently, he lifted his hands and grasped the heavy wool of her dressing gown. Anne slid her arms free of the garment and quickly divested herself of the nightrail underneath, glad that she only had one layer to remove. She wrapped her naked body in the warm wool again, fastened the belt and turned back to her husband. "Well done," she said, and traced a finger along his chin as a reward. He leaned in to the caress, his eyes fixed on her, waiting patiently for her next demand.

Her hand flattened and pressed, right over his heart.

A sound rumbled in his chest and he lay back, with Anne following to bend over him where he rested on the thick coverlet. One hand supported her while the other roamed where it wanted —reveling in the smoothness of his skin, the light rasp of hair, the feel of bones beneath muscle and flesh.

All this was hers, she reminded herself.

Simon's cock was already stirring, but it leaped to attention when she gripped it with confident fingers. He moaned, low in his throat. "Was that a question?" she teased.

"No, Countess," he replied.

She removed her hand and scratched one nail across the tender skin over his hip. He jerked in surprise. "Did I give you permission to say that?"

He gasped, eyes wide. "Permission to apologize, Countess."

"Permission granted."

"Forgive me, Countess." He gasped again when her hand resumed stroking up and down his hardened shaft. "Permission to thank you, Countess," he groaned.

Anne chuckled and swirled her thumb across the tip of his cock, which had begun to leak in eagerness. Oh, she had missed this—it had been so long. "Don't thank me yet," she said. She straightened and tilted her head, considering. "I need you on your hands and knees, facing away from me."

He obeyed at once, all but whirling over to assume the position she required, muscles and limbs stretching and straining with the movement. Anne filled her eyes with the sight of him, as satisfying as cool water in the desert. There were the strong arms with their dark springy hair and the thick male flanks, similarly furred. His belly was softer than the rest of him, and she knew it would soften more and expand as he aged, just as her own waist would thicken and her hips grow heavy with the years. Or maybe she would grow thin and wizened, as some of her great-aunts and grandmothers had done, with paper-thin skin and age-spots on her hands. She smiled to think of it—every wrinkle, every blemish a mark of another year survived, another experience filed away in memory.

He turned his head, a cheeky grin appearing beneath the mustache. "Permission to ask what the hell you're waiting for, Countess."

Anne laughed, but she recognized the apprehension that lay beneath his impertinence. "I have a strong suspicion you'll be asking me to go slower in a little while," she warned. She opened the jar of oil and dipped her fingers in it, scent rising around her in a delicate cloud. There was a definite pagan quality to this, as though she were an ancient priestess performing some carnal ritual, a mystery only to be revealed to the initiated.

And Simon was her sacrifice.

She moved behind him and set the oil within easy reach on the end of the table. He flexed just a little, shifting to maintain his balance. Anne bent over him, covering him with her warmth and pressing her smaller body against his heftier form. Her lips brushed against his backbone, there between his shoulder blades. His trust was humbling, a gift for her to cherish. "If you need me to slow down or stop, you are to tell me at once," she said. "No need to ask permission for that. Your countess's wish is to give you pleasure, not punishment."

His hot breath puffed out of him, a bellows beneath her breasts. "Yes, Countess."

Anne stood and put one comforting hand on his flank then examined him from this new angle. She'd long grown fond of the curve of his arse, but the complete geography of this part of him was still rather unexplored. The hair here was thicker and bushier, though not so thick as she'd seen it before—he must have trimmed it for her. Anne was touched by this thoughtfulness and decided he deserved a reward for his care. She knew where to touch him to make him jump—the puckered ring of muscle, darker than the rest of him and more sensitive.

A drop of fear briefly cooled her. Looking was easy—looking left her warmed but not burning, engaged but not imprisoned. Looking was safe.

All at once Anne was thoroughly tired of safe.

She took her oiled fingers and pressed them to that small circle.

He did jump, startled—she felt it in both hands. "Be still," she admonished, and began moving her fingers in gentle caresses, feeling him tense and flex beneath her hand, learning what speed and motion made him relax and what made him shiver a little. "How does it feel?" she asked.

"Good, Countess," he replied, and bucked his hips back a little against her. "Very good."

Anne shifted to stand a little to the left. The hand on his flank moved down and gripped his cock, stroking to match the rhythm her oil-slickened fingers set on his arse. He bowed beneath her hands, head hanging low, hips working slightly, panting and impossibly hard against the palm of her left hand. Anne pushed him further, speeding up a little, letting him relax into the tempo and let the pleasure spiral higher and higher—then, on the backstroke of his hips against her hand, she shifted slightly and slid one finger gently but firmly inside that hungry ring of muscle.

He spasmed around her and cried out, but she felt his cock pulse in her hand and knew that surprise was overmatched by desire. "Yes," she murmured, dropping her head to kiss the broad expanse of his back, tasting salt and sweat and need. "Very good." Little motions led to bigger motions and soon she was pumping that finger into him in earnest, her other hand working his shaft, all the prior urgency returning with reinforcements after the pause.

There was something so feral about this, so primal, as though she'd captured some great mythical creature and tamed him for her own amusement. And so responsive— she could move him with a touch, bend him with the pressure from just a single finger. His breathing grew ragged—Anne's own chest was heaving with effort and elation— and he gave a slight whine of the purest desperation she had ever heard. Her own body throbbed in counterpoint and with a gasp she pulled her hands away from Simon's straining flesh. He groaned against the loss and turned to look at her over his shoulder, amusement and accusation warring in his expression. "Not yet," she told him, licking her lips, trying to catch up with her racing heartbeat. "I'm not nearly done with you yet."

"Yes, Countess," he murmured, and the low sound of it went straight to her cunt. She quivered a little and walked away on shaky legs to where the dildo waited in its protective box.

She covered the polished wood with the oil, pouring it straight from the jar until it dripped onto the sheets by Simon's knee. Simon tensed when she touched it to him, but she gripped his hip with her other hand and held tight to let him know she had him. "I'm going to go slowly," she promised. "You will tell me if it hurts? If you want to stop? If you are uncomfortable in any way?"

He gave her one more heated glance, all but begging. "Yes, Countess."

Despite his willingness and the thinness of the wooden cock, things did not go easily at first. Anne worked him slowly, steadily, pushing the head in just a bit at a time, adding more oil as necessary, pausing now and then to slide her other hand up and down his shaft to keep him on that knife's edge of bliss. She focused and kept her ears open for every gasp, every sigh, every stutter of breath that meant she was moving too fast. At last the rounded head slid in and the ring of Simon's arse tightened around the narrow shaft of the dildo. "Wait," he said.

Anne went still at once.

Simon's torso heaved once, twice and a third time with steadying breaths. Anne rubbed circles on his back with her left hand—the one not coated in oil—and murmured encouragement. "Thank you, Countess," he said at length, with a shaky smile sent her way. "Please continue."

Anne wrapped her fingers around the base of the dildo, tilted it slightly, and pushed. It slipped in easily

Simon cried out.

She went still again. "Too much?"

"Oh God," her husband moaned, bending his head low and resting it on one bare forearm. "Do that again."

Anne laughed with pure devilment and repeated the gesture. Simon groaned, long and low, the pure carnality of it sending ripples down every nerve Anne possessed. She wrapped her left hand around his hips and began to work him with long, steady strokes, deep and slow and insistent. Each thrust drew one of those spine-tingling sounds from him, as though he couldn't help himself, as though he were an instrument for her own fierce pleasure. It was good—so very good—but she wanted more.

She paused again. "Turn over," she told him, punctuating the command with a sharp slap on his flank.

He obeyed, though the cock in his ass made him less than graceful. Anne stripped off her robe and let it fall to the floor while her husband spread himself out on his back, knees bent, cock up, the flared base of the dildo waiting for her hand to return.

"Yes," Anne purred. This was just how she liked him. Well, almost. "Hands above your head," she demanded, and watched the muscles in his arms and chest shift as he complied. His skin was slick and flushed, his eyes a little wild, his chest heaving with exertion, his face glowing with excitement and wonder... She had never seen anything more beautiful in her entire life.

And he belonged to her.

She knelt between his feet on the bed and he spread himself a little more to accommodate her. Then he simply waited, erect and aching and patient nonetheless. She leaned forward and loomed over him, supporting herself with one hand on the bed to her left, watching him breathe, humbled by his trust. "I love you," she whispered. "Now hold on."

She grasped the wooden cock and began seriously to fuck him.

He shouted so loudly she blinked and sent up a silent prayer of gratitude for thick walls and faraway servants. But she kept her hand moving, the wooden cock sliding back and forth like a piston. Every so often his body arched up and his furred chest teased across her nipples—at last she gave in to the inevitable and dropped on top of him, chest to chest, both her legs spread over one of his thighs, her hand still working hard at his arse. His hands stayed above his head, though the knuckles were now white and the fingers clenched into fists. Anne arched her hips and ground her cunt against his thigh, teasing him and herself before suddenly speeding up her thrusting hand and leaning up to his ear. "Come for me," she whispered, and bit down hard on his earlobe.

With a wild cry he tensed and obeyed, spurting helplessly between their bodies, his arse clenching so hard around the wooden cock that Anne was forced to hold still for fear of doing him an injury. It took a long time for him to stop shuddering, for his eyes to reopen, for the up and down of his chest to slow down from its breakneck pace. Anne looked down at the mess he'd made of both their nude bodies and was tempted to laugh—until she looked up at Simon and saw that he was weeping.

Shock stole the breath from her. "I'm sorry," she said. "So sorry. I got caught up."

He shook his head and laughed through the tears, finally bringing down one hand to wipe his eyes dry. "Don't be sorry," he said. "It was perfect. Terrifying and wonderful. Just like you, my dear countess." He grinned up at her while the panicked knot in her chest relaxed and dissolved.

Together they eased the dildo out of him. Simon collapsed back onto the bed while Anne washed the dildo, her hands, her belly, and Simon himself using a cloth and clean water from the basin behind the screen. He shivered a little at the water's chill. "Next time I'll leave it by the fire," Anne promised. He glanced up at her, and her confidence, now that she was just herself and not the countess, faltered slightly. "That is if you'd like a next time."

"I would," he said, so fast she nearly dropped the washcloth. He chuckled again and relaxed back against the pillows. "I really, really would."

Anne poured the rest of the water into the chamber pot and climbed into bed. Simon immediately wrapped his arms around her and she rested her head on the broad plane of his shoulder.

For the first time in weeks she felt warm. She felt safe and steady. The pit was so far away that she couldn't sense it anymore.

Before long Anne fell asleep—and for the first time in weeks, she dreamed.

CHAPTER 14

*A*nne had forgotten that morning in the country was so damn loud.

Not that London was particularly quiet, but the neighborhood she lived in as Countess of Underwood had a mild, polite assortment of manmade noises compared to other areas such as Covent Garden or Fleet Street or St. Giles.

But even those busy city places were grave-silent compared to Marlston at dawn. Anne woke up wondering just how many finches, sparrows, geese, ducks, warblers, larks, hawks, and kites were sitting around shouting in each tree. Six? A dozen? Only the owls seemed to have manners enough to keep silent.

She pulled the pillow over her head to muffle the noise.

A large hand tapped good morning on her shoulder. She waved in response but kept the pillow in place.

A low rumble reached her through her feathered shield, and it occurred to her how ironic it was to use a dead goose's plumage as protection from the shrieks of living birds.

And suddenly Simon's hand was on her breast.

Her nipple went instantly hard beneath his palm.

He felt it—she could tell because his fingers tensed a little and the hand began to move, sliding the warm hills and calluses over her tender flesh while his fingertips teased the soft skin of her breast above her heart. And then he cupped her, warmth seeping from his touch into her bones while his thumb made circles that left her shivering, desperate and hot.

Anne moved the pillow slightly to give herself room to breathe.

Simon's hand was replaced by his mouth and he curled his tongue tightly around her nipple. Pure flame shot from that point of contact and tunneled down into her belly. She couldn't resist arching her hips and spreading her legs, spurred by the need to move. Simon continued his leisurely tasting of her breast, while his hand skimmed lower, to her hip, and lower still to the curls between her legs. One long, thick finger slid against her clitoris and she opened wider to give him better access. He complied, stroking firmly against that hungry little spot. The pillow swallowed her quiet moan.

As if that were a signal, both hand and mouth disappeared. Anne felt echoes of his movement in the mattress beneath her— and then, with no warning, his tongue was on her clitoris, warm and slick and moving.

Anne tried to gasp, flung the pillow aside and winced against the light.

Simon lifted his head, amusement warring with uncertainty in his expression. He was rumpled and rough and unshaven, one cheek marked with a long red line where his pillowcase had wrinkled while he slept. "Good morning," he said. "Should I stop?"

Anne stole one of Simon's pillows, propped it beneath her head and let her eyes drift shut again. "Don't you dare."

He laughed, then put his mouth to better use.

Anne stretched her arms and legs out as wide as she could. The sheets were warm and soft against her skin, while her husband's mouth played havoc on her aching flesh. She pulled in a long, deep, lung-stretching breath and felt the blood rushing in her veins like a mountain cascade after the spring thaw. Simon slipped one finger into her cunt and hooked it, just *so*—and all at once Anne was coming, bowing up from the bed and clutching at the sheets and throbbing and gushing into her husband's mouth.

Eventually the waves subsided and she pulled Simon up for a kiss. Her own taste was sharp on his tongue and she smiled against his mouth. "Good morning to you too," she sighed.

He laughed and pulled her more fully into his arms. "Welcome back," he whispered. Anne shook a little but couldn't deny it— she'd been lost somewhere and it had taken her until now to feel as if her body belonged to her again.

And yet...

She pushed herself up on her elbow. "Simon, there's something I have to tell you."

"What's that?" He stretched out one elbow and rested his head on his hand, waiting with an arched eyebrow and the tiniest bit of a smile.

Anne refused to be charmed. This was too important. The howling wind from the pit seemed to fill her ears, its voice empty and deadly and cold. "I'm never going to be happy that I can't give you children."

True weariness lined his face then, the same weight she'd carried around silently for all those weeks in London. "I know," he said quietly. "I've been thinking about that." With a grunt, he pushed up in the bed so that he was resting on both elbows behind him, his face level with hers. "And what I've realized is—I don't need you to be happy about that."

Anne froze, surprised to find herself caught in the quiet eye of the storm.

Simon went on. "This is something beyond you, beyond me, beyond everything except Providence. I can't fix it. You can't fix it. But I'll be damned before I say that you have to like it."

"I don't like, it," Anne blurted, unable to contain the words for a single second longer. "I despise it. I'm so mad about it that rage could turn me inside out and leave my guts hanging out for all the world to see." She didn't see anything in his gaze but sympathy—maybe she hadn't made herself clear. "Simon, it makes me want to burn down the entire world, just because I can't have something I want. What kind of person does that make me?"

He only nodded. "I don't think I could trust someone who's never really wanted to burn down the world, for whatever reason," he said. "I know I've felt that. You can let this hurt become part of you if you want, because sometimes that's what grief does, when it goes right down to the bone. You can threaten to burn down the world for the next fifty years—and I'll be right beside you, every morning, offering to help you to stack the kindling. If that's what you want." Anne could only stare at him. "And if there's anything else you want, we'll turn the world upside down to find it for you."

"Why?" Anne whispered, stunned.

He gazed back at her, all his fierce devotion suddenly manifest, more tangible and real than the stone walls and ancient windows that surrounded them. "Because you would do the same for me," he said.

"I would," Anne said, because it was true. So this was what hope felt like. She had forgotten. It was a small thing yet, just a shoot pushing out from under the bleak, wintry earth, but it was more than she had expected. One flesh, the marriage vows had said—and the way he had offered her his body last night had proved it.

"So, Countess," her husband said as his grin returned. "What is it you want next?"

"Breakfast," Anne said at once. "But I'll have a more complete list for you later." The wheels in her brain were beginning to spin out the first threads of an idea.

Simon laughed, and breakfast was procured.

Two much more blissful days later, letters began arriving, sent on from London.

The first, lightly scented with roses, was from Lady Morley. Apparently Lady Audley and Miss Gilroy had been very busy at a recent house party, spreading word about the *ton* that the Earl of Underwood was hobnobbing with those of a debased social stature. That was precisely what Anne had feared would happen, but that worry felt so trivial and blunted now. After all, she was still a countess, still wealthy and married to one of the best men in England. She had let herself get confused by social expectations before and she would not let it happen again.

But surprisingly, Lady Morley was writing not to chastise but to voice her support.

It is so easy, she wrote, *for society to be blinkered in these matters. They see my title and my gowns and they take me for one of their own. They forget, if they ever knew, that my grandfather was in trade himself, digging canals all across the north of the country and building a shipping empire. When he succeeded in marrying my mother to my father—or rather, to my father's birth and bloodline—it was considered quite a scandal in its day. Many families refused her invitations for decades after. But by the time I was grown and wed to Lord Morley, they had forgotten all those bitter years. I was considered acceptable because I had grown up with the same wealth and luxury and manners that they all had.*

I still laugh, sometimes, remembering the summers we spent with my grandfather. He was the grumpiest of men when indoors, but when you got him outside, whatever the weather, his mouth would turn up at the corners and he would be content to sit, to walk, to do anything you wished as long as there was fresh air to breathe and perhaps a spot to sit and look at the hills rolling away to the horizon.

My grandfather died during my very first Season, while I was a hundred miles away and dancing with some duke or viscount or something. It broke my heart at the time, yet I could say nothing to any of my new acquaintance. I have never forgotten how lonely that felt, how angry it made me. I would not disown any one of those summer afternoons I spent with my grandfather, not if there were a hundred Lady Audleys to cluck and criticize.

But oh, look at me, an old woman waxing nostalgic about her youth. I am become a caricature, when I hoped to be a comfort. Please do give my regards to your charming husband, and if the rumors are true and you are to be reconciled with your cousin and your cousin-in-law, please do me the honor of introducing me. Anyone who can get Lady Audley this worked up has to be someone worth knowing, I think.

Yours,

Katharine, Lady Morley

The other letter, unscented and written in a far less elegant hand, was from Evangeline. This one Anne opened with some trepidation.

My dear Anne,

It is entirely wicked of you to resume connections with Hecuba when you know I must have missed her at least as much as you have. Or nearly, at any rate. Bertram and I were just returned from our honeymoon when the first rumor reached us. Or rather, reached me — Bertram rather misses a lot of the more pointed innuendo from Miss Gilroy and her friends. It happens so frequently that I suspect him of being dull on purpose. It certainly causes people like Miss Gilroy to talk to him less — which is why I am thinking of adopting the tactic myself. Georgiana Gilroy can be rather exhausting in large quantities. Everyone is always to be analyzed and dissected for their secret history, as if all her friends are pretty stones and she's always hoping to turn one over and find a spider underneath.

Does this mean we're all to be together at Christmas? We'll have to invite Bertram's mother, I suppose, but I doubt she'll come, not when Harold's house is so much more to her liking. At any rate, Bertram insists that I send you this plum pudding recipe, which he hopes your cook may learn before the holidays. He claims it's the best one he's ever tasted — and in such matters, you know, I am inclined to believe him.

Always,

Evangeline

So this was how scandals looked now, from these loftier

heights of wealth and privilege. When Hecuba and John had been caught in their affair, the subsequent disapproval had been instant and seemingly universal. The Pym family were nobodies, newcomers and therefore most easily cast out. But the Earl and Countess of Underwood had a lineage, an authority that people were loath to question even in the face of apparent misbehavior. It was presently convenient—but Anne, like Lady Morley, would never quite forget the cruelty of that first reaction, when she'd felt the full wrath of social criticism quite keenly.

She was glad not to feel it now. She knew it was a luxury but that was no reason not to enjoy the benefit.

Surely nobody ever deserved such cruelty, no matter their station. Anne had not always been fortunate, and there were many more like her. Or like Mrs. Walker, who was still isolated from the proper, public aspect of the world. Or Nicholas, whose resemblance to a man married to someone other than his mother was eventually going to excite comment and introduce trouble to his young existence. There were so many people who needed help. The idea she'd had that morning began to develop a foundation—but there were still things she didn't know, questions she didn't even know how to begin to ask…

As she stared out of the window, frowning in thought, her husband's gray hat rounded a curve in the path. Anne smiled and set her teacup aside with a click.

Simon had asked her that morning what she wanted, since she couldn't have children.

She thought she had the beginning of an answer.

Many years later

Two little ones came barreling around the corner and nearly took Anne's legs out from under her. They were no older than ten and virtually indistinguishable from each other, with short blond hair and angelic blue eyes and the red, red cheeks of excitement and activity.

"Careful!" she scolded, almost before she'd regained her balance. The two children gave her a look of mingled delight and fear and continued, running away to forestall further scolding.

Anne sighed and straightened her skirts. "Nicholas!" A teenaged head with unkempt hair poked out of a nearby doorway. Simon's brown eyes blinked at her from his son's face. "The Devitt twins have escaped Miss Adelaide's control again. Retrieve them for her, will you?" Miss Adelaide was as sweet-natured a woman as Anne had ever met, and wonderful with the younger set, but she had a distressing tendency to take her own lapses too much to heart. Anne had no patience for being endlessly apologized to. There were far too many things to do today.

"Yes, ma'am," Nicholas said, and loped off in the direction she pointed. He was more his mother's child than his father's, despite his looks—he had grown into a most even-tempered, polite and tactful young man.

Anne was counting down the days until he landed them all in trouble, and she knew Fiona was too.

She walked into the front office and found Nicholas' mother already there. Fiona supervised the day-to-day operations of the Underwood Children's Asylum, keeping watch over the building, the grounds and a veritable army of maids, cooks, groundskeepers, washerwomen, stableboys, and assorted other servants required for the care and education of two hundred children of every imaginable age and type.

So many children.

And they were all Anne's.

None of them had started out that way. Some had come in as infants, left on a doorstep or in a box or brought in by well-meaning but impoverished relatives. Some had come when they were nearly grown, lured by the offer of employment or training or just a safe place to spend a night. Some were illegitimate, others orphaned, but all of them were simply poor and unwanted. The dormitories were always crowded, but between them Anne and Fiona hated to turn away a child unless they had to. It was getting so that Anne was thinking of opening a second institution—out in the country near Marlston, perhaps, since many of the children would be interested in leaving London for one reason or another. To be closer to relatives in some cases—or to avoid them in others.

Fiona smiled, her blonde beauty undimmed by the passing of the years. Anne's own brown hair had more gray hairs now—the Devitt twins were responsible for at least a dozen of those strands —and she allowed herself a small moment to envy the way that golden hair masked the aging process. "Good morning, Fiona," she said. "Is everything ready?"

Fiona set aside her ledger and rose to embrace her friend. "The girls are bathed and dressed and fidgeting in the geography classroom."

Anne's lips quirked. "Nervous?"

Fiona sighed. "As always."

"Then I should go and have a word with them," Anne said. "Would you care to join me?"

"Thank you, but no. I have to catch up on the accounts—and we shall have to buy a pony to replace Buttercup. She falls asleep on her feet more often than not."

"Tell Bartlett to see to it," Anne said. Nicholas returned, flushed but triumphant, to report that the twins had been captured and returned to their proper places. "Send someone to tell me when the first guest arrives. Are you still both coming for dinner with Simon and me tonight?" Anne asked. Nicholas and Fiona nodded. "Good," she replied, and withdrew.

The geography room was a cheerful wood-floored space on the second story, facing the gardens and the fishpond that lurked behind the asylum. She and Simon had spent months choosing a site, back in the first days when Anne had proposed the foundation and its purpose. Gardens of some sort had been an absolute must, Simon had insisted, especially as she planned to house both boys and girls. "Girls you can raise in parlors and schoolrooms," he'd said, "but boys need places to explore and room to run."

"I expect the girls would enjoy that as well," she'd returned tartly—so gardens there were, available to all.

A circle of ten girls were in the geography room already, giggling and whispering and visibly thrumming with nerves. They all went silent and stood up to curtsey when Anne strode in the door.

She curtsied in return and looked them over. Clean, yes, and dressed in simple, pretty frocks. A lopsided ribbon here or there was nothing she needed to fuss about.

But what did need confronting was the fear in their eyes.

Anne couldn't really blame them. She'd been afraid in the same way once. She knew how to deal with it now.

"Good morning, girls," she said. "I know you must all be anxious about meeting the ladies of the Asylum Board and their friends, so I have come to talk to you a little and explain one thing in particular: these fine ladies are all far more scared of you than you are of them." The girls tittered and cast glances at one another. Anne allowed them their fun but pressed on. "It's true, however strange it seems. Some of them are afraid that you will be hungry or frightened or in dreadful need of a wash. Some of them are afraid that you will steal the very rings from their fingers —so control those fleet hands of yours, Jane."

Jane, small and mousy and unbelievably larcenous, only grinned in response.

Anne pursed her lips so as not to grin back. This was not the moment to encourage mischief. "What these ladies are really afraid of is that you will be different somehow from the children they've raised, from all the high-born children they've known in their lives. They are afraid to recognize you as human, because then they would have to pity you." Anne's eyes wandered from Maria, whose quiet eyes had seen more horrible things than Anne knew existed in the world, to Hilda, who had walked all the way here from Shropshire and chosen her own name and was the single most stubborn person Anne had ever met, to Lottie, who had been found squalling outside the stables when she was no more than four days old. She hadn't been expected to survive, yet here she was, hale and hearty. "But although you have not known luxury the way these ladies have, you have no need of their pity. You are strong, each one of you, far stronger than you yourselves know. You have worked hard for yourselves and your siblings and your friends, every day for all the years since you came to us." Jane's chin was jutting up proudly now, and even quiet Lottie was nodding along. "So today, despite all their privileges of wealth and rank and title, you are going to meet the wives of dukes and peers and Parliamentarians as equals..." Anne paused, grinned, and leaned forward. "And you are going to charm them right out of their skirts."

The tension broke with a laugh, a true one, and Anne could feel the volume of anxiety in the room vanish like mist under sunlight. They would be all right now, she knew. They would ask questions of Lady Morley and tell scandalous stories to the Duchess of Eider, who would be delighted and ask all the right questions. And if Viscountess Hambleton decided to come over all stern and moralizing, well, the girls could handle her. She was nothing so fierce as the Reverend Smythe, after all, who was as terrifying in the pulpit as he was absent-minded outside it.

Not for the first time, Anne wished she had the organizational prowess of Mrs. Bell to depend upon, but that august lady had cut off Anne's acquaintance when Anne had begun inviting Hecuba and John to visit in full sight of the *ton*. There had been a few lonely months, though never so lonely as when she and Hecuba had been estranged. And any rumors about Nicholas' parentage had been ignored in favor of the shocking, verifiable facts of Hecuba's profession. Yet over the years, even that distance was fading. Young Phoebe was currently off at finishing school, and every time she returned home she was more and more the young lady. Much to her mother's dismay.

Anne hid her smile and hushed her charges. "Are you ready?" she asked.

"Yes, my lady," they chorused.

"Good." Anne smiled, her heart filling. It was a strange sort of family, perhaps, this refuge for unwanted and unheeded children. But strange as it was, it was hers. And with the funding the board would gain from today's reception, it would grow and thrive. "Chins up, shoulders back," she said, "and show them why I'm proud of every one of you."

"Yes, my lady," the girls said again, and Anne ushered her troops out of the door.

ABOUT THE AUTHOR

Olivia Waite writes romance, fantasy, and science fiction, depending on the mood. She lives in Seattle.

In addition to her fiction, she reviews romances new and old in the monthly Kissing Books column for the Seattle Review of Books.

To get book updates, recommendations, fascinating research tidbits, and thoughtful longreads, sign up for her newsletter, which is sent out at the tasteful rate of every two months or so. You can also email Olivia at olivia.waite.books@gmail.com, or find her buzzing about on Twitter.

ALSO BY OLIVIA WAITE

A Thief in the Nude: A lady thief makes a deal with a gentleman painter for a series of scandalous portraits.

Generous Fire: A buttoned-up schoolteacher, a smouldering headmaster, and a steam-powered vibrator.

Hearts and Harbingers: A charming Regency sex fairy tale.

Happily Ever Afterlives: Two Regency paranormals in one! First, a damned lord and an ambitious demoness fall in love in Hell; next, an incubus and a debutante waltz across a London ballroom.

The Best Worst Holiday Party Ever: My shortest, sweetest contemporary with a sommelier heroine and forensic accountant hero. Original mulled wine recipe included.